THE
COOPERATING
WITNESS

Barbara Laken

V
Volume Publishing

The Cooperating Witness is a work of fiction. All incidents and dialogue, and all characters, with the exception of some well known historical and public figures, are products of the author's imagination and are not to be construed as real. Where real-life historical or public figures appear, the situations, incidents and dialogues concerning those persons are entirely fictional and are not intended to depict actual events or to change the entirely fictional nature of the work. In all other respects, any resemblance to persons living or dead is entirely coincidental.

Volume Publishing, 240 West 15th Street, New York, N.Y. 10011
A de Vera – Reyes Corporation Company

ISBN: 978-0-9792477-1-2
Library of Congress Control: 2008942928

Printed in the United States of America

Front cover illustration by Gary Breslin

For Glenn

THE COOPERATING WITNESS

This is a work of fiction, though many of the tactics used to collect taped evidence closely follow methods employed by an actual cooperating witness who, despite committing numerous felonies during his ten-year relationship with the Justice Department, remains a protected informant.

The interest the court fails to protect is the expectation of the ordinary citizen, who has never engaged in illegal conduct in his life, that he may carry on his private discourse freely, openly, and spontaneously without measuring his every word against the connotations it might carry when instantaneously heard by others unknown to him and unfamiliar with his situation or analyzed in a cold, formal record played days, months or years after the conversation...

> John Marshall Harlan II
> Supreme Court Justice
> Dissenting Opinion
> United States v. White, 1971

It is unclear whether the CIA notified federal prosecutors about the existence and destruction of the tapes before the matter became public. But one of the documents released Wednesday, a letter from Chuck Rosenberg, United States attorney for the Eastern District of Virginia, said a prosecutor in the...case "may have been told in late February or early March 2006" about the videotapes but "does not recall being told this information."

> *The New York Times*, February 7, 2008

> Now that the truth is out,
> Be secret and take defeat
> From any brazen throat,
> For how can you compete,
> Being honor bred, with one
> Who, were it proved he lies,
> Were neither shamed in his own
> Nor in his neighbor's eyes?

> W. B. Yeats

A Note on Format

The conversations depicted in this story have been transcribed from recordings gathered through electronic surveillance, except where otherwise noted. Portions of dialogue that follow the word "redacted" have been edited, or removed, from raw footage offered to the reader. Conversation found in unmarked tapes, and after the word "resume" has been preserved for the purpose of prosecution. All recorded material following the notation "tape break" has been irretrievably destroyed.

I

```
***FLINTLOCK DICTIONARY_ 13 june 2006_ telecommunications
hub 36_ routine aural traffic collection_ trigger word_ topic
alert_ forwarding criteria 1354092_ search list 1618***
```

... that dude deadhead Jamal happy anniversary cha-ching I said to Connie she should leave because pitch wait can you give me car deal I have say no to routine we need to **execute** the old country institutional purpose forecast looking like I do hey slut promotion with agency but the in the wondering stage I know it's expensive Germany overnight to the Pacific four days and who are spending sixteen hours through aloha stage input with **Wall Street** soon as possible rather behind Alaska sleep on deep in several times planning beforehand to carry out the sale on two locations what grade with did you get a chance to review if anything changes report back of all the places where did you go my hand hurt for profit to the deed and she said **praise be to Allah** ah that sucks to John and Shamed if I wanted **aircraft** going to scream who is going or somewhere you are going to get some sleep so I told my wife overseas I think I'll take it and the morning power curve for breakfast and the on employment **impact** creating leisure week market instead with initiative tell the processing officer in the Ritz morning thanks but I signed with the can you believe that but they were posting the attached opportunity in the third quarter for dynamic training and it rocks when effective how can you turn that down **aviation** mornings I told him arrive **in the next five days** in public for the fanny pack direct **weapons fire** personal can you believe the score team determined final section of the Chinese can't do the meeting on the future funding where the method that give your mother my love and takes with the fuck off you have table one this **could be killer** children in the academy make sure the restaurants operation survey best time would be taken for planning the delay switch with security tighter on the take the client list to arrive later on a motorcycle going green light red light with passport and schematic direct on how to dress and explain in detail to **bullet** point choreography concludes check watch split to the second all ready at the end of the line make it simple as possible with let their inhibitions below the knee this may be the easiest for the wire give me **potential targets** the most popular for kids in the chain brochure the travel agent said golf course good pay attention and precaution to every contingency where the ferry lands to how old is he **plan of attack** business and sheds new light on ask Dad all residents Thailand any link remains most wanted on the Internet for the I met the cutest guy last night in his minivan from Java listen on the final hours project director will have to numbers input if your mother says it's okay you can go out of the way with Humvee passengers **blasting** serious concern it's too soon to say any link exits but best time would be around seven p.m. they noted survey of young people presumed impact on reconnaissance helps consider because minds direct systems and they said they would can you think not about it I tell you **this will be the big one, God willing...**

AUTOMATED KEYWORD RECOGNITION FILE #126327: ECHELON special access interception center DODJOCC reports positive word spot output on international telecommunications between 843-991-5610 and a U.S. Person in South Carolina. Immediate human analysis recommended for processing and production.

Wiretape: U.S. Person # 16703
6/13/06 (:38) International

Hey, Rashid. It's Jamal. Returning your call.

Jamal! I was calling to see if you wanted to do a trip next Thursday. It's a stage input, going to the deed. It sucks, but you'll get your cha-ching!

Can't. I'm still in Sydney, working a few potential targets.

How's that going?

All right. Just blasting through some bullet points, putting together a plan of attack.

Hey, good luck with that. Just give me a holler when you're ready to fly aircraft again.

I'll be ready for small weapons fire, after this. I said to Ahn, if we can't pick up support in the next five days, we're gonna blow up here.

What does she say?

You know her. Always the optimist. Every time we go in she says, praise be to Allah, this will be the big one, God willing.

Well, I sure hope so.

Me too. We need to execute this the right way, if we want to make an impact on Wall Street.

My bet, you will.

This could be killer, if God gives us luck.

FEDERAL BUREAU OF INVESTIGATION

Date of transcription 6/14/06

On June 14, 2006 MAJOR SERGEANT RASHID DUKES was advised that the FBI received incidental communications intelligence from the NSA linking a phone in his office with a number belonging to a suspected agent of INTERNATIONAL TERRORISM. MAJOR DUKES advised the suspected dirty number belongs to MAJOR JAMAL HASSIM, a career officer, who currently flies C-17 transport aircraft for one of three reserve units MAJOR DUKES does scheduling for.

MAJOR DUKES stated that MAJOR HASSIM retired from active duty last year in order to spend more time raising funds to support a seaweed farm he and his wife operate on the Muslim island of Mindanao, in the southern Philippines. DUKES stated that HASSIM tried to encourage other officers on the base

to invest in this scheme, called BANGSAMORO SEAWEED – a publicly traded company, controlled by HASSIM, whose stated
goal is to encourage former members of Islamic rebel groups
to live peaceful, civilian lives processing and cultivating
marine products. MAJOR DUKES provided the stock symbol, possibly BSWE, and stated that HASSIM is currently in Australia
trying to raise money for another company he plans to operate in East Asia, called AQUA VENTURE.

HASSIM represented AQUA VENTURE as a private company
merging into a public shell that has applied for grant support and technical assistance from the U.S. Agency for
International Development (USAID), through a program called
Livelihood Enhancement and Peace (LEAP). A dramatic decrease
in USAID's resource levels over the past year has placed an
unexpected burden on all of HASSIM'S Southeast Asian operations. He is currently promoting these ventures to various
agents of FOREIGN POWERS, to procure additional funding.

DUKES advised that most of HASSIM'S American investors
are parishioners of the OLEL-ALBAB MOSQUE, and a few fellow
USAF officers who follow the Muslim faith, including DUKES.

The intercepted COMMUNICATION between MAJOR DUKES and
HASSIM concerns a four-day flying trip to QATAR. MAJOR DUKES
stated that HASSIM has TOP SECRET CLEARANCE and that he
prefers assignments to Middle Eastern combat zones. It was
assumed by commanding officers here that this was because
MAJOR HASSIM liked the tax-free hazardous duty pay associated with these missions.

Investigation on <u>6/14/06</u> at <u>Charleston Air Force Base,</u>
<u>Charleston, South Carolina</u>

<u>File#196C-ATL-236083 (108)</u>
By <u>SA DAVID BROWN</u>   Date dictated <u>6/14/06</u>

Tape 1A 6/14/06
Side A

[REDACTED]

The office of Assistant U.S. Attorney Patrick Fitzpatrick, please.
Okay, I'll hold.
Candy, what? Oh, no, no. Not now.
Do you really want to have this conversation while I've got the
Feds on the line?
What can I tell ya? Until I'm finished you'll just have to jones.

Hey Fitzie! My main man! Your sidekick Vartie dialed me up
earlier to say my services are needed again. I'll tell ya, I think your
boss is a little ambitious asking for three front page indictments
before the election, but you know what I always say, if you're up
against a deadline there's no one better than Conner Skilling to get
your business underway.

So tell me, is it true you guys got a pool going that I won't top my
best?
Listen, I can't tell you how to spend your money, but if I were

you I'd take the under on that.

You want to know what I'd recommend?

Right off the top of my head I'd have to say three months as a conservative guess.

And that's with me not havin' my trawl in the water yet.

Oh, Vartie didn't tell me you already got me a live one.

That completely changes the bet.

Okay, I'll take interesting but tenuous.

It's better than nothing — which you know is also fine — but a heads up is always appreciated. I'll take that any time, but if I got to go into the public and dangle a few apples, you know, I can do that too.

But hey, you're the quarterback on this. I'll happily work with the game plan you've already got before we contemplate any of our more imaginative moves.

I'm just saying, whichever way the story goes, I'm ready and prepared. You know me, I'm like the Energizer Bunny.

I beat down any path.

Just let Farrow know I'm dusting off my microphone, and ready for his call.

Hanging out and doin' nothin' in the middle of nowhere has been very nice, but I'm starting to get bored.

Oh, duh. Of course I know this is a secret initiative.

Tell your boss lady my lips are sealed.

Hey, and while you're at it, tell Miss Smarty Pants in control even though she's had me on ice these past three years, I've already forgotten what she'll never know.

Okay, don't tell her that.

Just say I'm honored to have the opportunity to be working for Justice again.

And while you're at it, you should make her aware I got a few things I'm developing in the white-collar department that she's welcome to use in case her guys in that division are slow.

If I'm correct about the one I'm lookin' at right now, there will likely be loss numbers you'll be able to use. You know, over five million, or something like that. I mean, it ain't gonna be Refco, but it's the kind of stuff that's juicy enough for at least some minor league attention. Who knows? Maybe something even better than that if it comes out on a slow day for news.

So let her know I'm offering that up as a token of good faith. You know, like a bonus for puttin' me back on the map.

Just give me a holler if there's any interest, and I'll follow up on that.

Of course, I remember the paradigm.
You have my word I'll stick to it like glue.
Record. E-mail. Confer telephonically at the end of the day.
And don't do anything until I get the okay from you.

FROM: CW 1
SENT: Wednesday, June 14, 2006 11:45:50 PM
TO: Agent Farrow

Cc: Agent Lossman, AUSA Patrick Fitzpatrick, AUSA Jason Varlet
SUBJECT: update

Greetings,

The following will serve to memorialize the events of 6-14-06.

At your request, I contacted Jamal Hassim telephonically and introduced myself as a wealthy financier, interested in information about the Aqua Venture deal. During the course of our conversation, Hassim mentioned he was conducting a group presentation tomorrow in Sydney and invited me to attend. I told him I'd fly in, but that I might need him to jet over to my place for an offshore "face to face" if I thought his business model was something I could work with, in order to introduce him to additional investors. During the course of the conversation I mentioned that I do a lot of deals with RODNEY FLITCH. Hassim had heard of Rod, and was very excited about the possibility of having a chance to present his scheme to one of Australia's most influential businessmen.

Tomorrow I also plan to "hook up" with Norton Merrick, regarding the Merrico Book Club deal. A stockbroker named Ritchie Gallo arranged for me to call Merrick at 3 a.m. my time, which is 5 p.m. in Boca Raton, where he lives. I asked him many technical questions concerning the proposed conveyance of a privately held convertible note to pay for various promotional purposes, during which time it was revealed to me that Merrick controls eighty percent of the issued and outstanding Merrico stock. This could be interesting for us. I'll let you know.

Regards,

Your favorite client

```
Communications Intercept: U.S. Person # 16703
6/14/06 (:26) International
```

JHassim 83 (8:24:23 PM): in the name of God, praise be to God and praise and blessings be upon his Messenger, it appears we have been visited with a blessing. A great man who has heard of our cause has promised to introduce me to his friend. He is very rich, and he is interested in our plan

STYoussof 95 (8:25:09 PM): dear brother, God has finally blessed you for your efforts and sacrifices

JHassim 83 (8:25:21 PM): that is my prayer

STYoussof 95 (8:25:35 PM): the gracious brother Abu Chowdry predicted you would bring us to our goal

JHassim 83 (8:25:41 PM): God permitting it will be so

STYoussof 95 (8:26:01 PM): God is the guarantor of success for every good deed

JHassim 83 (8:26:16 PM): purity of faith and the correct way of living are not necessarily connected to success

STYoussof 95 (8:26:37 PM): dear brother, God Almighty knows strength and kindness are not enough. That is why we soldier on

FEDERAL BUREAU OF INVESTIGATION
Date of transcription 6/15/06

On 6/15/06 SA ROBERT J. KIM, who was acting in an under-cover capacity (UCA) attended a prayer meeting at the OLEL-ALBAB MOSQUE, where he was introduced to SHEIK TARAK YOUSSOF, the mosque's imam.

The UCA informed YOUSSOF that he was new to the area, and wanted to get information about various options for worship before he picked a congregation. The UCA also told YOUSSOF that he was interested in supporting MUSLIM CHARITIES. YOUS-SOF then informed the UCA about his congregation's involve-ment with BANGSAMORO SEAWEED and AQUA VENTURE, and that both companies were constructed to support ISLAMIC INSURGENTS living on the island of Mindanao. YOUSSOF gave the UCA pro-motional materials about both ventures. He also informed the UCA that most of his parishioners are East Asian, and that many of them own shares in these companies.

The approximate time of the conversation was from 7:00 p.m. to 7:40 p.m.

Investigation on 6/15/06 at Atlanta, Georgia
File# 196C – Ga- 236083
By SA ROBERT J. KIM RJK/rjk Date dictated 6/15/06

FROM: CW 1
SENT: Friday, June 16, 2006 11:45:06 PM
TO: Agent Farrow
Cc: Agent Lossman, AUSA Patrick Fitzpatrick, AUSA Jason Varlet
Subject: The opening salvo

Greetings from Port Vila:

First: Some good news with Candace. The in vitro has finally worked.
Second: Wish me a happy birthday today.
Third: This will be a very busy week for us.

Jamal Hassim is scheduled to fly in on a private jet late this evening. I will send you a VERY COMPREHENSIVE e-mail after the series of meetings I have scheduled with him tomorrow.

During preliminary discussions, conducted after his presentation, I spoke to Hassim about the value of seaweed and fish crops to depressed economies in the southern Philippines, particularly on the island of Mindanao, where his proposed fish farm would reside. He provided press clippings that detail how funds from the Livelihood Enhancement and Peace Program (LEAP) sponsored by the U.S. Agency for International Development provide materials and technical support to Muslim rebels working for his seaweed farms and processing plants. When I expressed skepticism that jihadists could be tempted to give up fighting for the Bangsamoro mujahedeen based on the promise of employment, Hassim insisted that a valuable standing crop is the best deterrent to armed insurgency; though he did not dispute my contention that secure income cannot guarantee against continued militant activity.

In my opinion, the aqua farm deal that Jamal Hassim is currently trying to capitalize is a very well crafted scheme of global proportions, designed to secretly fund local and international terrorism.

I ALREADY HAVE ALL THE OFFERING DOCUMENTS AND MATERI-
ALS FOR AQUA VENTURE IN MY POSSESSION.

My contacts on Wall Street tell me that this deal has been shopped
around for over a year. Now that the Asian Development Bank has
reduced its forecast for Philippine economic growth and Standard and
Poor's has lowered Manila's credit rating again, any hopes of conventional
funding for Aqua Venture have become almost nil — which is perfect for
us.

The fun is starting on this. I'll keep you posted.

Computer Intercept: U.S. Person # 16703
6/16/06 (:12) International

Subj: Delayed Return
Date: Friday, June 16, 2006
From: Hassim Jamal M Maj AS/DOLP <jamal.hassim@charleston.af.mil>
To: "Dukes Rashid A Msgt AS/CCF" <dukes.rashid@charleston.af.mil>

Looks like I won't be back until Tuesday or Wednesday. E-mail info about
local flights leaving late next week, or put me on a four-day trip instead.

Subj: RE: Delayed Return
Date: Friday, June 16, 2006
From: "Dukes Rashid A Msgt AS/CCF" <dukes.rashid@charleston.af.mil>
To: Hassim Jamal M Maj AS/DOLP <jamal.hassim@charleston. af.mil>

We've got a four-day leaving on the 23rd into the box. There's a five-day

down range trip leaving on the 24th going through the South Pacific, stopping in the Philippines.

Subj: RE: Delayed Return
Date: Friday, June 16, 2006
From: Hassim Jamal M Maj AS/DOLP <jamal.hassim@charleston. af.mil>
To: "Dukes Rashid A Msgt AS/CCF" <dukes.rashid@charleston.af.mil>

I'll take the down range.

Tape 2A 6/16/06
Side A

[REDACTED]

> One, two, three. One, two, three.
> Okay, I think we're rolling.
> Candy, come on. Would ya lay off already? They're landing so
> you gotta get rid of the gimlet. It's gonna be like pulling teeth with
> regard to how we'll be able to proceed if the wife don't take to you,
> so have one more pop and then toss it, before they touch down.

> Listen, without getting more into this now, I spoke in great detail
> with Fitzie earlier today, probably around 11:00 our time, where I
> told him if we keep this going extremely smooth and I can actually
> deliver something in the next few days, that there's a presumption
> he's gonna call in a couple of favors with some contacts he's got at

the SEC.

I mean, not for nothin' but wouldn't you like to get off of this pile?

Yeah, well that's ditto for me.

Which is why as far as storylines go, we gotta present this in such a fashion that everyone feels comfortable. That's why I cracked out the Brooks Brothers blazer and told you no cleavage to show some commonality. 'Cause there's always a sales cycle with this and schmoozing, which will go much better if the wife thinks you're temperamentally similar from a social point of view. Remember, the key is to keep her busy and relaxed, so I can work one-on-one with the husband to establish some perceived credibility, and make my moves.

Nah, don't worry about me talkin' like this.

We've got a superlative post-production team.

They minimize all the stuff that don't directly impact the investigation.

So theoretically this discussion never took place, insofar as the legal aspect is concerned.

They'll just edit it out of the mix.

But now I've gotta watch it, 'cause we're seriously in play — so wave and give 'em a smile while they come down the ramp. There you go. See how easy? Look, the wife is waving back.

So mind your manners and just and follow my lead.

We got whales in the water here.

[RESUME]

Stop!

Stop right there.

You're under arrest!

Only kidding. Just one of my little jokes.

But seriously, don't move. Candy, why don't you go over and stand next to the Hassims. I want to take a picture to memorialize this event. Next to the wing is good. Just hold on to the little one if she don't want to get down.

We're very informal here.

Oh, that was great.

Now let me scoot in. I'm sure the captain won't mind if we ask him to play photographer for a minute.

That's good, buddy.

When you land back on the other side of the pond, tell Rod we say "thanks."

Now Candy, why don't you chat with Mrs. Hassim for a minute, while us men get the luggage and load it into the car. You can get her prepped on all the leisure activity you arranged, while we do a little advance work, and get a meeting schedule planned.

Right, smiley?

You're looking mighty dapper!

I was just telling the Mrs., after I introduce you to Mr. Hassim, you'll be able to say you've met a guerilla in a three-piece suit. And I say that affectionately, 'cause you gotta have a good appearance when you're pitchin' for a crew rigged out in camouflage, singin' Allahu Akbar. It's a necessary evil, when you're shoppin' for recruits.

Luckily for you, I don't care who I deal with.

I'm very adaptable.

Your idea is fishy, but I like it.

I've looked at it forensically — I spent forty minutes on it — and I said, "Hey, I love this thing!" It's a cute concept.

So I says to Rod, "This is clever shit. It smells good, and it's packaged beautifully. I need to see this guy on a private basis before he goes back to the States and sells it to a bunch of sub-cretins in Islip or some other armpit on Long Island, workin' outta a bullshit investment firm."

See, I have a retentive memory, so when I was watchin' you in Sydney, I was havin' flashbacks. I'm saying to myself, "Where did I hear this concept before?" Then I remember. This idea was shown to me by some knucklehead who said he might be able to do it through a neighborhood situation, which to me means "Mutual of Brooklyn" involved or something. Bein' that I'm not much of a planner, I didn't do a whole lot of due diligence before I seen you — which is why I only realize this when I'm just about home.

So I dial up Rod and says, "Hey, I need you to send Hassim over on your G-5. Your pilots can land on my airstrip. I'm only a couple of hours off the coast." And he's chuckling 'cause he's always yellin' at me about not thinkin' far enough ahead in time, which between us girls, is more natural for him, bein' one of them corporate types. But Rod is like a brother, so after he gets done scolding me, he says, "Conner, if that's what you want, I'll make it happen for you." To which I says, with regard to how we should go forward with Mr. Hassim I think it would be the best thing to do. It's always better to deal direct, mano a mano...'cause obviously we don't want to discuss this ad nauseam over the phone.

So when you says to me, "I don't know if I can, owing to the fact I got commitments with the force and the family and all." I says,

"What's the difference? You're almost here already. Tell 'em you're sick, or that your Aunt Matilda died. If you want, I'll make the call. And if you have to, I've got no issue if you say to me, 'Conner I got to bring the wife and the daughter along.' "

When you leave, they'll be sayin' I'm the best activities director they ever knew.

We got beachfront and warm bloods.

The kid can dig sand castles and take a soak in my Jacuzzi.

And as for your better half, she's all set up too.

We got her a tour of the island and a massage at The Palms — so there can't be no beefs about nothin' to do.

This way we can conduct our business nice and quiet, in a way that's very discreet. It's always better to meet in a private manner, before I present you to my contacts, and my friends on the street.

No, no. We don't need your wife in on the action — at least initially. And I say that affectionately, 'cause she's very attractive, for a girl of her kind.

I'll tell you what — she'd bring a big number off one of them Philippine websites that advertise brides.

Whoa, whoa, whoa.

Don't get your balls twisted.

I meant that as a compliment, not for you to take offense.

When I saw her in Sydney, I says to myself, "This woman is very informational on why so many of her brethren live in them mountain jihad camps — and she's overtly scholarly on how many carp and what kind of pens."

But for now, we got to keep her undercover from a protocol point of view.

See, the head scarf and prayer beads will actually scare off my investors — which is why you have to be the face on this — at least until we get your farms up and running — or her some new clothes.

So for the moment, we're not gonna mention it's the wife, more than you, at the helm of this ship. I just need to make sure we're on the same page here, because this has been met with a much higher level of reception than I remotely expected. Meaning, I knew it was gonna be good, but this is good squared.

Listen, I hear ya. I can see why she'll be somewhat disappointed, her bein' a key player in structure of the business and the concept and all. What can I say? You'll just have to have a sit down this evening and explain this is a temporary situation. There'll be plenty of time after we get you financed for us to phase her in.

Besides, I've already got 'em waitin' in line on this one — chompin' at the bit.

What I mean is, she don't need to tell me no more information, or give me any more spiel. You're already on the menu, as I would so eloquently say.

The appetizers have been served.

Like, it's a done deal.

FEDERAL BUREAU OF INVESTIGATION

Date of transcription <u>6/16/06</u>

Source, who is in a position to testify, provided the following information:

At approximately 8:58 p.m., Pacific Standard Time, source participated in a consensually recorded conversation with JAMAL HASSIM and his wife, AHN HASSIM in Port Vila, Vanuatu.

Source subsequently contacted SA Farrow to report the time the recording device was stopped, at approximately 9:34 p.m., after source drove THE HASSIMS from a private island airstrip to a guesthouse on his farmstead, where THE HASSIMS plan to stay for a few days.

Source advised that this initial meeting was successful, with more substantive discussions planned for tomorrow.

Investigation on <u>6/16/06</u> at <u>New York, New York (telephoni-cally)</u>

File #<u>196C-NY-236083</u>

By <u>SA Kevin Farrow</u>   Date dictated <u>6/16/06</u>

Tape 3A 6/17/06
Side A

Jammo! Welcome to the Big House, or "*haos timba*," as we call it in the local dialect.

Let me show you around while Mingo prepares our lunch.

Wood houses are as rare as 1099's in Port Vila; this one bein' a former navel hospital from World War II, when Melanesia was the base of Allied operations for the South Pacific...which means you ain't the first Air Force major to land on my airstrip.

I got pictures of Bob Hope standin' next to a C-47 transport right where you came in.

Look. Betty Grable too.

Screw palms and stranglers took over almost everything after 1945, except this house, and a few Quonset huts. These islands fell off the map after that — except for clever little guys like me that come here to structure situations that are, for lack of a better word, a little bit beyond the norm.

So when I sold the horse farm in Jersey, I says to Candy, "I got this doofus with a coconut plantation that owes me money on a stock trade. What d'ya say we take his place? It may be sittin' on top of a tectonic plate, but at least it's on the part that's movin' west. It's got fifty acres, a herd of Angus, tennis courts and a swimming pool. If you get bored you can hop over to Fiji or Melbourne. They ain't that far away. Just look at it as a one-off trade with an interesting storyline that we can use until somethin' better comes our way."

At least the guy who owned this place had good taste, even if he was a little bit of a scurrilous character. The floors are teak, the kitchen appliances top of the line, and you can't beat the views. We got lagoon, bay, harbor, valley —

Mountains too.

Don't worry, Mount McDonald has been dormant for a hundred years. If you stay an extra couple of days, we can drive up to the crater rim.

What looks like smoke at the top is just rain shadow and fog. On the way up you'll see orchids you can't find no place else on earth.

See, in Vanuatu the key word is creative.

Like, we can do whatever the fuck we wanna do, except maybe commit a murder.

Of course, there are detractions. The help is, and I say this affectionately, only a few notches up the evolutionary ladder from Neanderthal.

And believe me, the people I hire are the cosmopolitans!

The average native gauges his net worth in pigs, wraps his dick with a palm leaf, and thinks he ain't dressed without head feathers and face paint.

Most of these Shemendricks still live in straw huts.

My doghouse offers better accommodation!

But the labor is cheap and reliable, even if it looks like it just stepped out of the Stone Age.

By the way, tell your wife Mingo only wears that bone through his nose on special occasions. Since he's the first in his family to wear pants and a shirt we have to give him a little discretion.

At least I stopped him from showing off his missionary pot. They don't boil Presbyterians anymore, but lets just say, there was a time when holy rollers from the mainland were considered big game.

The islanders called them "*Jisas mit.*" They hunted 'em, slaughtered 'em, and hung 'em upside down to dry, then served them grilled and stewed. If they wanted to bring a housewarming gift to another tribe they'd give 'em a leg or an arm, as a sorta "how do ya do."

Now that's a tactic for your mujahedeen! Instead of shooting at them army bastards they could slow roast 'em, then offer 'em up in gift packages — like them baskets they send out around holiday time.

You're laughing! I'm serious!

Like, "Hey, you want to fuck with us? Come on down! We'll have the paprika in hand along with the basting brush, and the shrink wrap ain't far behind!"

But seriously, before we set the table, I want to make it clear that I'm not looking to make lamb chops from the lamb, I'm looking to make wool. You know, we're not gonna make hamburger out of the cow, we're gonna get milk and dairy products on it. We have a few situations here that are looking for an annuity, with reasonably strong discretion to make an investment.

They'll invest in anything within reason, but its got to look good.

So I've already had a series of meetings, telephonically, with a plethora of potential investors. And they've gone splendidly.

The material you faxed me, along with the resume, went over better than I thought. And I knew it was gonna go well, 'cause I never have a meeting unless I have an idea of how it's going to go.

And it just went better than expected, so the groundwork is set wonderfully.

In addition, we have a couple of swinging dicks flying in that I have a great deal of potential influence with.

The first is the Trade Minister of Indonesia, who will be arriving here tomorrow. His name is Sheik Abdullah Ali. And he is a near and dear friend, very influential in the Muslim community, with charities and whatnot.

Now essentially he's a fund manager. He manages in an offshore capacity, like I do, and he just invests for himself through a bank he recently purchased in Java, which is part of the central banking system there.

So we'll have an informal meeting with Ali tomorrow, when he flies in with Rod, my Aussie. He's the colleague of mine who you met in Sydney, at your presentation. He's got the largest insurance company in Australia, with a couple of billion dollars discretionary in his investment fund. I've talked to him at length, and he's reasonably predisposed to move along with this particular venture.

Now, I know you understand the mentality of Australia, since you visit several times a year.

It's the country convicts started. So it's in the blood.

As I like to say, *there*, the prisoners got the keys.

And Indonesia, what with your background supporting local mujahedeen, is a perfect marriage. Sheik Abdullah is a fruitcake just like you.

He likes to invest in startups that help support the local economy.

You'll be like two peas in a pod.

But most of the corporations we're friendly with — most of them are knockaround guys and union guys. They're friends of the family, if you understand what I'm saying.

We've got carte blanche with these guys 'cause they're all wired up, from pillar to post. We got an open door, all rigged.

See, I understand your frustration in getting this project off the ground. You've been nurturing this fucker for three years. Sophisticated investors should be saying, "Wow, this is a great idea," instead of saying, "I ain't gonna get involved with a bunch of rag heads in some third-world country with a shaky economy, no matter how smart the concept is."

Not for nothing, but my screen saver says, "I'd rather be lucky than smart."

After you get to know me, you'll see that my specialty is creating luck; the kind you never dreamed you could have, 'cause I never bring things to people they say no to.

I bring it to where the answer is likely "yes."

Look, you're much more expert than I am on ocean pens, and

I, what for my own, being a clever little fella, may not have the knowledge you have about tilapia...but make no mistake, I know how to catch big fish.

Take my Aussie, for instance. He saw your show at the Sheraton, and he says to me, "Conner, aquaculture in the Philippines? You could sit at home and run an aqua farm out of your spare fucking bedroom. It ain't rocket science. It's easy. It's cheap, and there's potential for a good return. But if we get a blippie a year or two down the road, like they have with milkfish production right now — down twenty-five percent from last year — there's nothing to ameliorate the blip."

I know, I know.

Milkfish are grown in ponds, where pollution is more dangerous to production intensification.

That's what I was trying to help you with when you were doing your Powerpoint. I mean, you had your forty people there, even though they were somewhat of a moribund crowd. So I sat, and I asked you questions that you needed to be asked — without you asking — while you were putting up the graphs.

I was like, "Hassie, Hassie!"

I kept flipping the book open with the Powerpoint, and pointing to the graphs — "Not that graph, this graph! Stress oceans, not ponds!"

I'm sure you must have been saying to yourself, "Who is this devilishly handsome little guy sitting at the head table pointing to the right charts?"

Now that you know me a little better you can see I'm a big stickler on efficiency.

Plus, I've been watching your seaweed operation for two years —

which is very impressive. And I says that to Rod, I says, "Jamal is already generating good returns with his seaweed farm, so he's proven he knows how to run a successful business; and remember, this new operation is all gonna be in open water, raising ocean fish."

And I basted him, and marinated him, and I brought him back to the fold, 'cause I showed him the instrument I devised to bring your business public, and he saw the craft and the handiwork. It's masterful. A work of art.

So I showed it to him, and he says, "It's a beaut."

He was tickled pink.

My background?

I started out working for some screwball who sold used cars while I was puttin' myself through school.

By the age twenty-two I got started in the car leasing business. That business developed into a fifty million dollar top-of-the-line firm. So the leasing business was spinning off so much free cash that I opened a trading firm.

I mean, we sat there and owned some of the largest firms in Manhattan. I wish we never did, 'cause I'd have no compliance issues, which end in four months or six months, or whatever the case may be. But what I do for a living now, I'm more in the venture capital business.

Deals like Aqua Venture come to me on a private basis. And I can fund stuff anywhere from five hundred thousand to five million. When deals get more than five or six million I gotta bring in the cavalry.

I say, "Rod, I need three mil...four mil."

And I have a pretty extensive Rolodex of guys of this ilk who are worth a hundred million on up to God knows what they're worth.

I also have connections with overseas banks and fund managers who, shockingly enough, get along wonderfully with me.

And there are other wealthy individuals and entities that are willing to put something in there if we can justify a deal.

I'm hooked into London money, Swiss money, and fund managers that are near and dear to my heart, with accounts in Monte Carlo, Switzerland and whatnot. They're sitting there ready to deploy money. They look to me for advice because we've buried a lot of bodies together. And we're friends, a long, long time. We usually collectively get in things, and use each other's contacts to build a better company.

For instance, theoretically, let's say a year ago I got involved with Aqua Venture. We'd be busting balls — all of us — using our collective contacts to increase revenue, which, you know, builds value.

Well, finally, Mingo! I was beginning to think that you went into the rain forest to spear our lunch.

I specifically told him no pork, but maybe we'll be able to tempt you with some rousette au vin — that's fancy for flying fox in wine — a local favorite.

Just think, when you go back home to Atlanta, you can tell the guys in your squadron that you went to a place where the culinary specialty is sautéed bat. If you weren't so damn fussy we'd be serving mangrove oysters and homegrown escargot.

I mean, not for nothing, but you got more rules about food than this rabbi I knew. I used to say to him, "You ain't lived till you eat trayf" but he was one of them zealots, just like you.

Mingo! Why don't you pull out the seat overlooking the coconut groves for our guest?

It'll give you the best view of Mele Bay, where I'm sure you've already noticed the boat traffic is rather — primitive.

This is probably the only island chain in the world that still uses hand carved outriggers as its primary form of transportation. Imagine that! Eighty-nine islands connected almost exclusively by one and two man paddleboats!

Most of 'em are uninhabited volcano peaks and coral reefs, that don't have nothin' on them except caves and colonies of Cormorants anyways, which can make them nice little hideaways for all kinds of skullduggery, but that's about the extent of what they're worth.

You can never tell when an underwater lava flow will belch up another one, or blow one of 'em away. On the Rim, as we like to so affectionately call it, destruction and uncertainty are a normal part of our day to day.

Just ask my buddy who plays blackjack at the Palms. He lost half his net worth at the roulette table last week!

Now that Mingo's moved our table under the banyan, I'm gonna have him pour you a glass of Latour.

I don't give a shit what your religion says, my religion says, "Get rich or get drunk tryin'." Besides, the wife ain't here, so we don't have to worry about her getting all hot under the hijab about you takin' a taste.

By the time she gets back, at the end of the day, you'll be long past detection, as I like to so cleverly say.

Hey, I'm like you, I'm the kind of guy that doesn't typically stray from tradition, except where there's a plausible exception — of which this is undoubtedly one — since I ain't never made a success-ful deal yet where a toast hasn't been done.

So raise your glass, and let's have a drink.

Here's to my guys pulling the trigger and makin' Aqua Venture a household name in just a few weeks —

What?

Well, lookie here. The island travelers, home early.

Hey, Candy, what happened? You weren't supposed to be back for another couple of hours. It's barely one o'clock.

I guess I can understand how a four-year-old can only take so much fun and frolic, before she's gotta come back for a little bit of a rest.

I knew they wasn't back so quick 'cause Candy ran outta activities for them to do. I always say, if you have any question of my sales ability, she's the living testament. I'm a cute little fella, but let's face it, I wouldn't be able to land a statuesque blonde like that without a great sales pitch.

And she's a good sport. While we chat with Rod and Ali tomorrow she's gonna take your wife and daughter for a swim at the Mele Maat Cascades.

No, no. Ya got to explain to the kid that Mele Maat ain't no water ride — it's just a waterfall with a swimming hole.

And tell her, Candy will take them over to Devil's Point to watch the porpoises and feed the tigers if there's time. There are tons of tiger sharks hanging out in the coral reefs off the south west coast, the reef fish being easy picking. They're like, "Oh la de da, let me just mind my own business here in this gorgonian fan," and before they know what's happened, they're sucked right into some hammerhead's digestive tract.

It happens that fast.

Bang. And the party's over.

So much for the meek inheriting the earth.

If you need further proof of the fallacy behind that concept, Mingo can take you on a hike into the evergreen forest behind our

house and show you stone tables where they used to fillet the fri-
ars...and I ain't talking chickens!

Now wait a minute, you take me wrong.

Mingo! Let me have an ashtray please.

No, no. Hassie, let me say this, 'cause there's a dichotomy I
need your wife to understand, as in we're all deadly focused on the
same goal — just from different sides of the camp. So when she says
to me she doesn't feel comfortable being kept at a little bit of a distance, I'm gonna tell her what I said to you, "The only way your
story is gonna get told is by designating me to deal with the dirty
details," as in, I'm the best guy to take the lead on this for you. I can
sit there and put on a bow tie and drink the best Cabernet, while
promoting a business bein' operated by people who could never
entertain investors in a normal kind of way.

Which is why I was just tellin' Hassie, "We're gonna pretend
we're out tonight for a cocktail meeting — so let Mingo pour the
wine — and when no one's looking I'll just switch out yours for
mine."

See, I had to give him some practice, so that when we go out
socializing later on a men's only basis he can stay above the fray,
while at the same time giving the appearance of having a multi-
dimensional brain.

This is why I said we need you to take a little bit of a backseat
until the ink is dry. Which in my expert estimation will be in just a
few days.

After that you'll have all the time in the world to sit down and
discuss your position.

Okay?

I don't understand what you don't get.

See, I'm tryin' to help you put some fresh focus on your program, which, in my opinion, can only happen if you step back, at least for the initial part of the pitch. And if you give me a minute to explain, I'll tell you why that is.

For one, it's a bad idea to be talking to potential investors about putting twenty-five percent less fish in your grow-out nets, which I notice you have a tendency to do.

I understand it's to protect the environment — and that's very nice — but it's not a good idea, since most of my contacts are gonna hear that and say, "Why should I put my money into an operation that compared to the competition is gonna earn twenty-five percent less at the end of the day?"

That's how people think.

I don't care what you've heard about the doing well by doing good trend.

It doesn't work in the real world, as I think you're starting to see.

And I'm telling you this not because I want to be right on this issue — which I wish I weren't — but because I need to say this to you as a friend.

And let me tell you something else. That tape you show with your father givin' a tour of the facilities has got to go.

Listen, I'm not trying to insult you — but don't you see how that might give the appearance that you're running some kind of rinky-dink operation? I mean, not for nothin', but it makes it look like you're sellin' stock for some mom and pop store.

Hey, you can stand there all day long and tell me how he's a community leader integral for recruitment and re-training, and I'm gonna tell you that falls under the category of information we call, "don't need to know."

Alls you want your customers to focus on is the bottom line. They don't need to see how you dry the seaweed or who fillets your fish — which is why I was about to tell your husband that in addition to your old man, that guy Abu Chowdry has also got to get the heave ho.

It don't matter that he's been your plant manager for ten years.

Or your cousin —

I don't care if he's Jesus fucking Christ.

Alls I know is he gives the appearance of someone who looks threatening from a cultural perspective. Like he could be makin' tapes for Al Qaeda when he's not makin' 'em for you. And I say that outta the greatest concern, 'cause I understand he might not be the one responsible for that, but that's the impression he incites.

Well, I'd say the fact that you can't see that explains why you've been on the road for the last year and haven't raised a dime.

And I mention that with great affection, because I like your idea.

Remember, I'm on your side.

See, what you're forgetting, and I was just about to say this to Hassie before you arrived, is that the audience you're currently appealing to ain't from them bleeding heart programs you're used to dealing with, like the World Bank or the Asian Development Fund. My people are only interested in rate of return. They don't care how many starving families you've brought down from the mountains or how many shoeless children are sifting garbage outta dumps. They're no more concerned about that than they are about living conditions for factory workers in Jakarta or Shenzhen. The point is, you have a tendency to emphasize the wrong aspects, which I can appreciate due to your emotional involvement, but that don't make it the right strategy for bringing in capital. Which, from what I can see, if you can't achieve relatively soon will leave you without the ability to help anyone in the end.

That's where I'm coming from.

Do you understand?

You wanna go back to the guesthouse and discuss it privately? Fine.

Put the baby down for a nap, and talk it over one-on-one. Just remember to keep your eye on the time.

I didn't have a chance to mention this yet, but Hassie needs to meet back up with me within the hour, so I can drive him into town for an appointment we have at a local bank to set up an offshore account.

See, now that you're aligned with me, you're gonna need that for the crossover to handle the profits, once we get your stock in play.

And I say that with great confidence, because I got a lot of big time people waiting for me to say good on this — but they'll only invest in a confidential environment, which is what we're gonna set up for you today. That's why I told the manager at ANZ, "Don't even think about leaving for your conference in Tauranga until my friend Hassie comes in and acquires a number in-house." To which he says, "No worries, we can take care of that pronto, so long as he comes down before the end of the day to take the registration out."

FEDERAL BUREAU OF INVESTIGATION

Date of transcription 06/17/06

Source, who is in a position to testify, provided the

following information:

At approximately 12:00 p.m., source participated in a consensually recorded meeting with JAMAL HASSIM at his home in Port Vila, Vanuatu. The conversation was initiated at approximately 12:00 p.m. and ended at approximately 1:10 p.m., Pacific Standard Time.

Source subsequently contacted SA Farrow and SA Lossman and advised that during conversation JAMAL HASSIM (HASSIM) stated he was eager to find investors with criminal back-grounds, and wished to combine his business interests with those of other ISLAMIC MUJAHEDEEN in INDONESIA. Source advised that based on comments about wanting to see Christians "roasted," he believes Hassim is presently trying to raise capital to fund terrorist attacks in support of worldwide holy war.

Source advised that he has been asked to arrange a meet-ing between JAMAL HASSIM and GREG RUSSELL, an offshore bank-ing consultant with ANZ BANK, so Hassim can open a secret numbered account at ANZ to avoid U.S. scrutiny. Source advised that Hassim also wants to purchase pre-existing "shelf" corporations through ANZ, in an effort to further disguise illegal transactions.

Investigated on 6/17/06 at New York, New York (telephonically)
File# 270d-NY-262295 196C-NY-230660
By SA Kevin Farrow   Date dictated: 6/17/06

Tape 3B 6/17/06
Side B

Let me navigate us through the commercial district, so you can get a view of the sunset without having to peek between duty-free shops.

Hey, you monkey, get out of the way!

These fucking island natives got no respect for cars. I drive this for my own pleasure, not because any of these jungle bunnies know the difference between a Mercedes and a Montero.

And I say that with all due respect, so don't pull out your solidarity card and get all finicky like your wife.

Are you kidding? They love me here!

I'm like a king.

You saw how they scampered around when we went to the bank. It was, "Mr. Skilling, how can we serve you? What would you like today? You want to start up a new multinational corporation? We'll set up meetings with government officials, introduce you to regulators and create legal structures so you can operate, tax-free, anywhere in the world. You want to domicile a going concern? We'll back it up into a pre-existing company, with a group of yes men on the board, ready made. No more social security, withholding tax, or extra employee expenses for you!

Want to protect assets from creditors?

Have your offshore company buy products from one country, then sell them to another, with profits accumulated tax-free?

How about a new hundred-foot Broward with no tariff from Uncle Sam? Just sign a few papers. Here's a numbered trust account, with a ready-made trustee.

If you pick up any pressure, he'll be the guy sayin', 'go fuck yourself. It's none of your business who my client is.' "

I'm glad you took the paper work.

You'll want to fill that out soon, so that we can get our project underway. My bankers can incorporate in less than twenty-four hours, so it won't hurt too much that you took a temporary delay.

I still say you should have done it today, but take your time — just not too much of it — 'cause our swinging dicks are comin' in just twelve hours, along with a dear dear friend that I haven't mentioned yet, who I'm going to introduce you to tonight at the casino.

He runs a hedge fund with three hundred million in it.

This is a very, very close friend. So keep it quiet, just between ourselves.

'Cause this friend mandated me to find the perfect investment. It has to be dressed nicely, and it's gotta have some real basis of economic reality.

He looks for situations with a shot to work that are extremely cleverly packaged. The stuff I do with him has to have much higher levels of sophistication and perfume and flavorings 'cause he only invests if nobody knows from nothing.

Nice and quiet, under the radar.

Ah, there we go, finally out of town.

It's hard to believe three blocks can take so long, but when you're dealing with sub-cretins who have never seen more than ten square miles or ten bucks in their pocket you have to put up with a certain amount of attention.

You're right. I'm the "*bigfala*" around here.

That's what they call me. And you know why that is?

It's because I know how to create stuff with layers of insulation so in case we hit a hiccup, no one's got an enforceable beef. That's why I construct little quid pro quos with characters like you, so you can pay for my services in an offshore brokerage account, in a very cute manner. That way we're always guaranteed to get the end cut on our meat.

Let's pull up to the shoreline for a minute.

I don't know about you, but I never get tired of watchin' the sun drop over the harbor at the end of the day.

Candy says that's 'cause I like situations with high predictability. And I don't disagree. That's why I'm so successful. I make sure to hedge my bets, so when it comes time for the payout, I'm always first on line.

And people that work with me on a personal level understand that, which is why I can get them to stew on stuff they might not have a high proclivity for.

Take my buddy who you're gonna meet tonight —

He wasn't even thinkin' about your fish stock until I admonished him to consider it, after which you could hear him tapping the buttons of the calculator in his brain.

It's like I always say in regards to my investments, "The run-up is important, but the real finesse depends on controlling how the deal goes down." Ya never want to construct an instrument that ain't firmly under your control, 'cause then you could end up like those nincompoops out there that run their boat smack into a limestone cliff that got pushed up on a fault line, where yesterday thirty feet of water used to be.

Boom!

A total wipeout.

We'd better pull outta here and work our way toward home before it gets dark.

As you saw on the way down, the roads can be treacherous.

Like right here for instance, all rutted dirt and sand.

I told Chief Tanna he has to fill in some of these potholes, especially by the hairpin turns.

You're gonna meet him in a few minutes — he's the head muckety-muck of the Namba tribe. They own the road we're driving on and all of the land north of the hotel district, including the sixty-two acres under my farm.

We're working to change that, but when you're dealing with pre-hominids, modernization takes time.

Right now, only ruling clans, like the Nambas, are allowed to hold title. Everyone else can only lease — the average lease being seventy-five years — which these knuckleheads figure is the life span of a coconut tree.

And you see how they run things.

This tree trunk has been layin' here since cyclone season.

Don't worry. I've slipped around it hundreds of times.

One thing you don't have to concern yourself with is me lettin' myself take a slide off the ledge of some mountainside. I'm much too crafty for that.

See?

Back from the edge, and on the road again without a scrape.

Now, what you have to keep in mind when you meet Chief Tanna is that even though he may look like a primate, with my cleverness and your cleverness, he can sit at the head of our board as a head of state!

Let's face it, if your deal blows up and the shit hits the fan, the statute of limitations is five years. It would take the SEC at least that long to figure out how to interview him in Nambese, and until then we'll have discretion on his signature.

Oh, no. Don't take me wrong.

I agree. Aqua Venture is highly visible and credible.

It smells like rose petals.

If it didn't smell good we'd all get pinched.

But any deal can turn stale. That's why they put airbags and seat-belts in cars. Nobody anticipates wrecking their car. I was just trying to construct your collision insurance. And from what I can see, you need that, what with the active recruitment of terrorists —

Okay, "separatists" if that's what you want to call them — as you're planning to do.

I mean, not for nothing, but what happens if one of your crew gets implicated in a bombing in Bali, and says, "Yeah, I came down from the training camps up in the jungle, and was clandestine for a year, working fish cages off the coast of Sulu for an American company on the New York Stock Exchange while waiting for final instructions."

I don't care how vigilant your wife's family is about screening. Nothing is one hundred percent.

In fact, I would argue the familiarity you say is an asset has the opposite potential, in that it makes it more likely for them to over-look threats. And let's say that happens?

What then?

See what I'm trying to say?

Well, here we are.

Eriki village.

Home of the Big Nambas.

You're right.

Someone should call *National Geographic*, but the question is, would they come?

This ain't exactly the easiest place to find, and, not for nothing, but these natives sometimes look at you the way my German Shepherd looks at a rib roast.

Don't worry, there's no danger anymore, unless you insult them, and I'm gonna make sure you don't do that.

That's why I brought you here.

With you potentially doing business locally, its important that you observe the local custom of carryin' your own kava cup.

I keep one in my jacket pocket at all times.

It's just a coconut shell with some carvings on the side, but it has tremendous importance to the people here. Even expats like me and my buddy Malik, who I'm gonna introduce you to tonight.

See, in Melanesia, it's custom to drink a cup of kava at sundown, which I was about to offer you when we were down by the beach, and then I remembered that I hadn't gotten you one yet!

Since kava only brings luck if the cup is blessed, its important to get your cup from a chief, who can put the right spell on it, like, "Let the bearer of this cup be surrounded by many pigs," and stuff like that.

Just be warned that on our way to the naka-mal, which is a sort of hut where they drink this stuff, you gotta make sure not to stare at the women preparing the dance circle over there. Some of them have nice tits, but if they think anyone who's not a blood relative is checkin' out the merchandise, they'll hide behind their headdress in shame.

You definitely don't want to go in to meet Chief Tanna while his women are coverin' their war paint with hawk tails, and I say that in a cute, kinda offhand manner, 'cause what they're really getting ready for is the annual grade-taking ceremony, where the chief will demonstrate his wealth by destroying more than half of it.

I'm not kidding!

In a few hours old Tanna's gonna stroll past that lineup of boars over there and brain a bunch of 'em with a club.

He'll tap the lucky ones with the tip of his mallet to show they get to keep on living — at least 'til next year — when he decides on them all over again.

But more than half of 'em lined up over there thinking their biggest worry is when they're gonna get their next serving of oats, don't know their more immediate problem is if they're gonna have to sacrifice their skulls to Chief Tanna's version of pork barrel politics.

See, with the Nambas, greatness is determined by destruction of assets.

The more pigs you kill for the village to eat, the bigger man you are. So tonight there's gonna be a lot of pork chops goin' down.

Personally speaking, I'm like you. The only chop I'm looking for is an aggregate of a forty percent earn in a numbered account.

I'll put my meat cleaver in that any day.

No, of course — I didn't realize.

If I knew women wearin' only skirts was an offense to you, I wouldn't have brought you up this way.

But we're past them now, and hey, look!

There's the chief!

He's the one with the thickest bark belt, and the purple palm leaf wrapped around his johnson.

You're right. They certainly do let it all hang out here.

But we're all friends. And believe it or not this guy is like a Supreme Court judge.

And that's no joke.

He's a justice of the peace, the head delegate for his tribe, and the biggest power broker on this island — with an appointment good for life.

So smile, look past the face paint, and remember this is a privilege.

Not many outsiders get invited to a kava ceremony.

And no, it ain't alcohol, so you can't say you ain't gonna imbibe.

It's just a local root these nut jobs pound into a drink. And it's very popular here, even though it tastes a little like the bottom of my shoe.

So hustle up and follow me into the kava hut, 'cause the chief's waving us in with his staff.

Now remember, this is a big honor, so after he presents you with your shell, toss down the kava like a shot. The chief will grunt and bless you with a few spells and it'll be official.

You'll be one of us.

What?

Say that again?

Okay, okay.

Well, bro, we have a problem.

The chief says you need to take off your skullcap before we can begin the ceremony.

Well, let this be the first time since you've been in the Reserves then.

Only before you sleep?

How about before you meet the men who are about to change your life?

When there's hundreds of millions at stake you have to make a few compromises. We won't tell the wife.

And let's not get carried away here. He ain't asking you to choose between your God and his; he's just asking you to recognize his power, which is signified by him being the only man wearing headgear.

Maybe it ain't right, but what is?

Is it right that Christians in Manila withhold capital investment from Muslim islands like Minandao, then blame people there for joining militant groups to defend themselves against gettin' starved out and marginalized?

Is that fair?

Everyone's got a right to stand up and fight for their place in this world, I know you agree, but you ain't gonna be able to hack up any support unless you demonstrate you're a player.

By that I mean someone willing to bend a few rules to get to the grand prize.

Like me.

See, there's a sort of division of labor here.

My division is to drive money into your business. Your division is to make a good appearance, and maximize credibility.

I've got 'em nibbling at the water already on this one, but you're the one who'll have to make them bite.

They ain't gonna go for the bait if you act like an Ayatollah, or one of them by-the-book holy rollers, which is why we had to take your Mrs. outta the picture on the presentation aspect of this, which I know you understand.

So I don't wanna hear the chirping, like I don't wanna hear, "Oh Conner, I would but my mullah might get mad."

What you have to remember is that the only faith that really matters is my faith in you, 'cause there are very few investors that are gonna give a flying fuck about fish farms for Philippine insurgents. So you can give me all the happy horseshit you want about the LEAP program and international support. The bottom line is that without my contacts, Aqua Venture will exist on your prospectus only.

In other words, as they say in Brooklyn, you're gonna have to cough it up.

Like, I can't have you sit there and introduce you to any of my friends so I can press them in a very smooth manner to get them on your program if you're not on mine. Which means taking off your kufi, downing a couple of shells, and schmoozing in a normal way, by entertaining my associate with me over dinner tonight, then going into town and rolling some dice.

There. Was that so bad?

Just stick it in your back pocket and I'll tell Chief Tanna we're ready.

Hey chief! *Man ya I dring fulswing!*

Okay, sweet pea, just sit right here on this tree stump, and remember not to laugh when the chief and his men do their little stomping and shuffling routine. They need to get those nut rattles on their ankles jingling before your initiation is official, which, by the way, when it's over, gives you honorary status amongst the Nambas. You'll be an associate just for allowing them to shuffle around you in their dancing masks.

Now sit tall and show respect.

Hear those slit drums approaching?

That's the women beating time outside the naka-mal, so that the chief and his men can have rhythm to dance by.

There they go!

I'm gonna step back and enjoy the show.

Remember, drink the kava in one gulp — and try to drink it all.

It's considered bad luck if you don't take it down in one swallow.

From: CW1
Sent: Saturday, June 17, 2006 6:45:36 PM
To: Agent Farrow
Cc: Agent Lossman, AUSA Patrick Fitzpatrick, AUSA Jason Varlet
Subject: KEEPING YOU VERY BUSY...THE STORY UNFOLDS

Greetings from Port Vila;

The following will serve to memorialize the events of 6/17/06 as they have occurred so far.

I spoke to Norton Merrick this morning about his NASDAQ stock, MBAC. We had a very cordial conversation, during which he stated that "he would like to figure out a way that it would be worth my while" to participate in the promotion. I will have a better appreciation of his value after I read his prospectus and the "Fed Filings" over the weekend in great detail.

Jamal Hassim arrived back at my house around 3:00 p.m., after which I drove him to the Port Vila branch of ANZ bank, where he engaged in a lengthy conversation with bank personnel about secret offshore accounts, tax evasion, and various methods of concealing international transactions. He left the bank with the necessary paperwork to apply for a variety of offshore financial instruments, including secret trusts, dummy corporations, and covert, preregistered "shelf companies," created to disguise ownership.

During the course of our drive to and from the bank, Hassim divulged the following information:

a. He plans to actively recruit Philippine terrorists to work for his proposed fish venture.

b. That these terrorists could likely be associated with global terrorist attacks while in his employ.

c. That his terrorist employees could strike outside the Philippines, in
   Bali, for instance, with explosives or other means of deadly force,
   and that it is not unreasonable to assume that some of these
   employees would use work on shoreline fish cages as an excuse to
   deploy from guerilla camps in the mountains of Mindanao to establish "sleeper cells" amongst the general population.

At the moment, Jamal is back at my guesthouse preparing to accompany
me for dinner in the hotel district, where I will introduce him to one of
my contacts. By the way, I notice that it's almost June 18th in New York.
Happy Father's Day! I hope you get plenty of gifts.

THERE IS GREAT STUFF DEVELOPING HERE FOR YOU. I will keep you
posted in real time. Let me know what you want me to do.

Tape 3C 6/17/06
Side B

Just let me grab a cigarette. There, now, where were we?
The pigs! Still with the pigs?
Really, you have to get over it.
It's the way of the world, man!
Some of God's creatures have to be sacrificed not because
they're bad or necessarily deserving but because they happened to
be in the wrong place, or because someone with power didn't hap-
pen to like the way they look or have use for them anymore.
Simple as that.
That's what they call fate, my friend, and don't let anyone tell

you it don't operate the same for us as it does for a lineup of hog-tied boars.

You of all people should know that, after all them trips you've made overseas, carryin' ammunition and caskets back and forth.

Let me tell you a story.

Back when I was in the car-leasing business, before I opened my own leasing company, I had a quota to meet. So being that I have more angles than a geometry teacher, I end up with all my contracts lined up before the middle of the month, ahead of my boss.

And this fuckin' guy, you'd think he'd be thankful.

But no — he accuses me of rigged deals, like, helping clients cheat on bank applications and stuff like that — which of course, I would never do.

But he makes these accusations, and brings them to corporate.

And you know what they say?

They say, "Sorry Conner, but we'll have to let you go while we have an internal investigation."

Can you believe that shit?

So they kill my business, and take my client list, all because of this fuckin' guy's impression.

They fucking brained me.

So I went to a lawyer friend of mine, and I asked him under direct cross-examination, okay, what could be done, if we could sue them, and if we could use, say, defamation of character. And you know what he said?

He says, "Conner I see this every day. Someone in power has a beef with you, or an agenda that your destruction will enhance; you might as well kiss your ass goodbye. Nine times out of ten the party with the power and the purse strings wins, no matter who's wrong or right."

You know that yourself.

Do you think that you'd still be begging for investors in Aqua Venture if you were a Catholic, looking to install fish cages off the coast of Manila?

We both know the answer to that, which is why I'm only going to introduce you to colleagues who are predisposed to your position, like my buddy Malik el-Tiberius, who, though he's from Brooklyn, actually has a brain lurking in his fat carcass.

And he's a former Nation of Islam, Black Power guy.

Hung out with Malcolm X and all those dudes.

Now he's a quiet investor who runs three hundred million out of ANZ Bank.

But he grew up on the right side of the tracks — our side.

So we're gonna do a little socializing with him tonight before my Australian and my boy from Indonesia jet in tomorrow.

See, Malik and I used to beat each other up for our lunch monies back in New York. So he's like a blood brother.

You could say we're neighborhood friends.

Now, just so you know, Malik has already been pre-tenderized on your situation, meaning I've already put him on the rotisserie and roasted him golden brown — which is his natural color anyway — especially with any kind of Islamic brotherhood — help the Taliban sort of deal. God forbid it should have a decent curriculum!

What do I mean by that?

I mean you don't have to go through all the blither and the blather about investment schedules, company philosophy, and rate of return.

He's pre-sold.

Which is probably a good thing, being that this island air has you sorta knocked out.

Nothin' that another shell won't fix up, though.

And don't even think about refusing, 'cause if Malik sees you don't partake, he's gonna say, "I thought you said this guy was tight with the chief," and go yickity yackity all over the place about how he won't do business with someone he can't break bread with.

With Malik, customer relations is key.

Meaning, you got to schmooze him while I baste him, before we marinate, and set him up to broil.

See, stopping at a few naka-mals on the way to wherever you're going is a tradition here in Vanuatu.

It's a cultural thing.

Since Malik has been living here a few years now, it's a ritual for him. Every night at the Red Light he tosses down a few shells and shoots the breeze. Since it's on the way into town, I said, "Hey, take a load off. We'll pick you up on our way down to The Palms."

It's the least I could do.

See, there's a dichotomy here you've got to understand.

It's my job to access who's gonna meet who.

It's like, I make the marriage, and you show up to take the vows. Meaning, you don't have to put your pitch hat on, 'cause what we basically have with this is a sort of fait accompli.

See, Malik relies on me exclusively for investment advice, 'cause he may have dough, but he doesn't know the difference between common stock and livestock, him being a former cop and all.

Yeah, that's right, Malik el-Tiberius used to be detective Melvin Smalls with the NYPD — Treasurer of the Detectives Endowment Association, head of the Brooklyn gang unit, and all that sort of stuff.

When he was with the force we could be going down the street on Broadway with a needle hanging out of our arm and an open bottle Jack Daniels in the front seat. Only in New York could we do that, you know, do anything within reason.

Once I went through the tunnel I could have a problem with that.

But Malik, he's the best. And I'll tell you what, he still has influence with the force.

In fact, I told him to order you a complimentary detective's shield with your name on it. He says, "No problem. I asked you to find me an investment whereby I could support my people and you came up with the mother lode. I needed a wrench, and you came up with a Snap-On power tool set."

It was the equivalent of me saying, "Hey gimme your car, I need to use a car to go to the train station," and you drivin' up with a CL 600 Mercedes.

Now before we go in, there are a few things on the table we need to discuss, which I think are better for a private discussion, no disrespect to Malik.

As you know, I've been very active in coming up with some prospective proposals for giving Aqua Venture more visibility in the marketplace.

It's a menu that we want to go over.

Meaning its not one idea, it's basically, do you want chicken? Do you want steak? Do you want fish? And let's pick. Whether we want a lamb chop, I don't know.

I've been spinning this one around, and not for nothing, but before I present my colleagues who are in charge of the trigger on these things with basically a little bit of a cafeteria, you know, "pick door A, B, or C" — and there's no question they're gonna pick a door — and I have a very good thought of what that door is gonna be.

But before I do, not to be crass, I gotta ask, what's in it for me?

A commission?

How about a kick?

I'm from Jersey, kickback is fine by me.

Let's say, with my influence and cleverness, I get Malik to invest a ten million dollar tranche into your business. I would expect a commission, or kickback, through a little maneuvering with an ancillary company, of say, ten percent.

Well, there's always room for adjustments, and I'm not negotiating.

I got to drill for a little minimum-maximum here though, 'cause Malik ain't just some common moron.

Like I told you before, he used to be the treasurer of the Detectives Endowment Association, which he isn't anymore on account of his retirement, but he still has connections to the union, and they're very receptive to his advice. So Malik has already offered to bring your deal to his old union buddies for consideration, and since they're not extremely sophisticated investors, and because he has such a good reputation with them, there'll be a de minimus amount of skepticism involved.

Plus with their investment advisor being down six percent last year. Seriously, Smith Barney, down six percent —

They're looking to make some independent investments.

But these guys, you know cops, they all like to live a little over their means, so Malik and I will likely have to take care of some of these characters, you know, with trips to Las Vegas, a few five hundred dollar dinners, a little traveling expense money — stuff like that.

You'll never see it, and you'll never know about it, but this is why I've got to have a little bit of an evergreen tree.

No, no. Don't get me wrong, we won't run amok.

We can't drive drunk down the fund deployment highway.

And we don't want to do anything stupid.

Malik's guys can't help out with any Federal beefs.

State, you know, I can be going a hundred and fifty miles an hour, and I'm not getting in a problem in the city of New York, but they got no influence with the Feds.

So we do everything real careful.

I just don't want any misunderstandings, because we're going to start to go down this path and generate a lot of money; and if the detective boys like your project there could potentially be referrals, like to the Health and Hospitals Union, the Court Officer's Union, the Lather's Union — outfits like that — that have a board of trustees that are chafing at the bit to find lucrative investments they can justify to the membership.

Well, here we are, the Red Light.

You can't make a move with your seat belt on, Jiminy.

And no, you can't wait here. We've got to go inside.

Besides, a little fresh air will do you good.

By the way, for tonight's meeting you can use your real name, but for tomorrow it's better to go incognito.

It's just that Jimmy will sound better to my Indonesian than Jamal, 'cause all these big time international Muslims are discreet investors. For obvious reasons, they want to know that you're not running around raising any eyebrows back in the States.

Malik is the same way.

He only goes by his Muslim name when he's with his brethren, of which I'm an honorary member having known him for twenty years, but when he's opening doors with anyone else he calls himself Melvin, just to keep everything comfortable.

Like when he worked for me, when I still owned a broker-dealer on Wall Street, after he left the force — he couldn't call customers, like Mrs. Magilacutty in Kansas and say, "This is Malik el-Tiberius, I've got a hot tip on Microsoft," 'cause she would hear his name, and slam down the phone.

Excuse me partner, two shells please.

Gimme your cup.

There.

Let's toss one back before I take a look around for Malik.

As you can see, it gets kinda crowded...and it's hard to make anything out clearly, what with only torches for light.

What's that?

Your mouth feels numb?

You got to buck up, 'cause we got a long night.

And remember, we're all friends, so relax.

Our main concern is to make an introduction.

Malik don't need to know all the gory details.

He don't wanna know.

What he knows about you is enough to set the table.

Seriously, how many Air Force majors are there out there lookin' to help enemy combatants?

I know, separatists, freedom fighters, mujahedeen, fellow Muslims — whatever you want to call them.

But seriously, how many officers are there that come from your background, that he can look in the eye, who are conversant in the Koran, affirmative action and all that jabber, that a guy like me can't delve into.

And I think I told you, he grew up in the projects too.

The only difference being he's a full-on brother, not a half Filipino like you.

But that don't matter.

All he needs to know is that I'm gonna get your stock in play from a payroll perspective, with a broker-dealer outside the range of U.S. jurisdiction, which I'll explain later, because here's our man now.

Mallie, Mallie! Over here!

Hey, Jack, put up another couple of shells!

Round two, ya punk!

From: CW1
Sent: Sunday, June 18, 2006 3:15:45AM
To: Agent Farrow
Cc: Agent Lossman, AUSA Patrick Fitzpatrick, AUSA Jason Varlet
Subject: THE PLOT THICKENS

Greetings from Port Vila:

This correspondence will serve to summarize the continuing events of Saturday, June 17, 2006.

Tonight Jamal Hassim enjoyed a six hundred dollar dinner at Rossi's, and a few hours gambling at The Palms. During the course of the evening, I introduced him to Malik el-Tiberius (AKA Melvin Smalls), a dirty cop turned Muslim convert, who has expressed interest in furthering radical Islam through investment in Aqua Venture. I have taken the liberty of recreating an excerpt of the night's events in order to establish a flavor for the threat these men pose to national security. I've done my best to accurately represent the recorded conversation. I have inserted a (UI) notation for the unintelligible portions of tape, which I will fill in later, based on my recollection.

CS: Hey Jamal, did ya notice what I ordered? Milkfish!

JH: We call it Bangus in the Philippines.

CS: How do you say it? Banus?

JH: No — Bangus. B-A-N-G-U-S. Bang-us.

CS: Very slick, Hassie. I love it! Bang-us. I'll tell you what, the next time I want to order up something hot from Sulu City I'll say "Bang down some Bangus," and I'm sure your guys will get my drift.

JH: They'll think more highly of your palate if you order the grouper.

CS: Grouper. I'll remember that, which won't be hard, 'cause Hassie's a kind of grouper, meaning all the true believers gather around him when they have any questions on all that Muslim mumbo jumbo he's an expert on. It's like I was telling my friend Malik, "If you want to know anything about the Koran ask Hassie, cause he's an Islamic scholar."

JH: I wouldn't say that...

CS: That's my good buddy Hassim, always playing schmucko. What he's not telling you is that he's certified.

JH: As a pilot.

CS: Don't let him kid ya. I heard his wife say he's a recognized expert on the Koran — as in he memorized the whole thing. He's an official hajji...

JH: Hafiz. I'm a hafiz.

MT: So you know all the verses...

JH: I used to. I'm a little (UI)

CS: I'm gonna bet a hundred dollar chip that Jamal still can cite you a textual answer on any information you have a desire to know. Like jihad. Ask him any question on that subject and he's gonna stand up and deliver like a broker that gets a dollar stick on every share.

MT: A hundred dollar chip don't seem like a lot.

CS: Oh, what the fuck, make it a deuce.

MT: Five hundred.

CS: That's a little rich there, Malik-ie.

MT: That's my price.

JH: I really have(UI) to make these (UI)

CS: I keep telling this boy, he's got to loosen up.

MT: He looks (UI).

CS: Oh, he ain't anywhere near your loose-o-meter. Or mine. He's as straight as a poolstick, aren't ya kid?

Waiter: Excuse me sir, may (UI)?

CS: By all means. Hey Jamal, don't cover (UI). Now, come on Malik, question number one.

MT: Okay, does the Koran support international Muslim unity against Western domination?

JH: I'm sorry, what? (UI) Can you say that again?

MT: I said, does the Koran support international Muslim resistance to Western aggression?

JH: When the territorial integrity of Islamic lands is threatened, the Koran instructs us to "Prepare against them whatever force you can muster."

CS: (banging table) Ha! See, I told you! He's a Koranic savant!

MT: Not so fast. I got two more questions.

CS: Okay, shoot.

JH: Do you think we can get them to lower the lights in here? I'm starting to get a headache.

CS: Waiter! *Laetem out. Tispun, man we I save (UI)*

MT: All right. Does the Koran support the Sunni or Shiite interpretation of Islam?

CS: What kind of question is that? That has nothing to do with jihad!

JH: "Hold fast to the rope of God all together and fall not into disunity," that is what Mohammad said. I believe he would have been disappointed with our contemporary divisions.

CS: These are softballs! You're not even trying to challenge him!

MT: What's wrong with that? I'm the one who stands to lose.

CS: This is not fun. I'm gonna ask the last question to put a little spice in our contest. Jiminy, you ready? Here it goes. Does the Koran specifically state that holy war is justified?

JH: "Jihad" means "to strive" in the face of persecution and oppression.

CS: Hey Malik, after we raise two hundred million to invest in Aqua Venture, we should run this guy for Congress. Can't you just see it now? The honorable Jamal Hassim from the state of Georgia! With evasive answers like that he'd be perfect.

MT: With no textual reference! I win! Five hundred beaners, right here in the palm!

CS: Jamal, my man, don't let me down here. I know stuff about holy war has gotta be in there somewhere and you were doin' a little cover-up in a very politically correct manner just to be polite. But now you've put me in a sort of bad position with my boy Malik here, so I'm gonna ask you again in a very direct way to pony up for the big guy who's gonna put Aqua Venture on the map, so this little Q and A ain't gonna make me add an extra five hundos to the expense account tonight. So I'm gonna ask you again, where in the Koran does it state holy war is justified?

JH: It could be said that there are (UI) sometimes referred to as "war passages" in the Koran which (UI) call for holy war against all unbelievers. (UI) interpretation. Mohammad said, "Let there be no hostility except to those who practice oppression," In my opinion (UI)...

Let me just fill in some of the blanks on that last passage right now, while my recollection is still fresh. Hassim said, "There are over a hundred war passages in the Koran that call for holy war against unbelievers. I believe in Ayatollah Khomeini's interpretation, that it is the Muslim duty to defend Muslim interests against the Great Satan by all means possible. Mohammad said, 'Let there be no hostility except to those who practice oppression.' In my opinion Western policy has been consistently oppressive toward the Muslim community since the days of Saladin, which entitles Muslims, under Koranic law, to retaliate with whatever methods and weapons are available to them."

This is only a small portion of the night's activity. Other important developments include:

   a. Jamal Hassim's agreement to pay a ten percent "kickback" to me, so
      that I can have money to bribe New York unions and other poten-

tial investors, in order to lure them into the Aqua Venture scheme.

b. Hassim's willingness to do business with a corrupt detective.

c. His desire to obtain a fraudulent police badge with his name on it.

d. His use of the alias "Jimmy Hassim."

Special Alert:

The names of certain fish are likely used as code words for activating terror cells and initiating potential attacks. Any intercepted communications in which types of fish are discussed between Hassim and any of his co-conspirators should be regarded as possible terrorist chatter.

THIS IS POTENTIAL HEADLINE MATERIAL, WITH NATIONAL AND INTERNATIONAL IMPORTANCE.

Let me know how you want me to proceed.

Regards,

Your Favorite Client

Tape 4A 6/18/06
Side A

[REDACTED]

Do you see what time it is?
You're supposed to be up and dressed.
Yeah, well I can see you're not feelin' too good.

You're lookin' a little rough around the edges.
Like you've been ridden hard and put away wet.

Ohhhh. Is that what it is?
You couldn't sleep because of your conscience?
How many times do I have to tell you, it's all part of the cover —
this do-gooder save-the-world crap. That's what they do to take your
eye off the ball, so you don't recognize their true purpose.
And don't roll your eyes — 'cause I know this for a fact.

Let me tell you something: What we're working on here is a
national security investigation with a capital N, so don't sell yourself
on the assumption you can treat this situation casually, like it's some
local by-the-numbers pump n' dump gig.
This is the big leagues, sister, and you're in it up to your eyebrows from an operational point of view. No different than when we
set it up for your father to slip on the grape, when I told you there's
no way Pathmark ain't gonna come up with a settlement irregardless
of the circumstances, 'cause it's gonna cost six figures to defend.

And I say this with concern, to remind you that you don't want
to be putting yourself under great scrutiny, which will likely happen
if this project gets derailed.
My point is, don't go acting like you're independent pursuant to
the execution of this particular transaction, 'cause it won't be to your
advantage if it fails.

Oh, come on. Now you're gonna get all teary-eyed?
See, this is why when you ask me for a few lines tonight I'm
gonna say no.
It fucks with your emotions, and then I gotta deal with this.

That's I why I said from the beginning no more until after this particular operation is finished, which I let you talk me out of, and now look what we've got.

You blubbering about that woman and her little brat like they're normal, everyday people — which they're not.

And, by the way, that's been confirmed by some very, very in-depth investigation outta Washington, which says these guys are about to make moves of a global dimension on some very politically connected stuff.

So put that in your crack pipe and smoke it while you fix yourself up.

[RESUME]

Hey, hey! Look who's here!
Well, good morning to you too, Jiminy.
Oops, we'd better say good afternoon. I've been so busy all morning assembling promotional packages for Malik's union guys, I barely had time to notice you were MIA.
He was real impressed with you last night.
He called me up this morning and said, "This guy, this fuckin' Hassim, he's like a poster boy."

Oh, oh, I'm sorry.
I didn't notice your daughter.
Cover her little ears.
Hey, what's her name again?
Come here, Aseelah.
Don't be shy.
Give your uncle Conner a kiss.

Put it here, right on the cheek.

That wasn't so bad, was it?

Okay, there we go.

I put you down.

Why don't you go find Aunt Candy and tell her it's time to take you to feed the porpoises again?

My wife was just sayin' how your little one really enjoyed the trip to Devil's Point.

For today she's booked a "girls only" tour on a glass bottom boat that takes off from Eriki lagoon. From what I understand it's supposed to leave soon, which is a good thing, 'cause we have a lot of business to discuss.

You're not sure what there is to discuss after last night?

I'll tell ya what, you may not have seen it, 'cause you don't really know the guy, but I've never seen Malik so excited.

I ain't kiddin'.

He's already in fifth gear on this thing. He's just busting at the seams about it, callin' all his contacts, and he tells me he's already starting to get referrals now. By tomorrow he could potentially have ten unions lined up. He has a lot of connections with unions in New Jersey and Westchester County, besides the ones he knows from New York, and he's ringin' them all up.

Listen, just between you and me, I think he's more excited about you being a brother than he is about your stock.

Once he heard you were, and I say this affectionately, a man of color, he didn't even need to see your paperwork, since he trusts me implicitly.

He says, "Conner, I'm not looking at it. Just walk me through it."

So I did, and he said, "It's perfect, I'm in."

And he loves the idea of you helping your Muslim cronies get themselves out of poverty and all that gobbledygook.

It couldn't be better.

I knew I was making a match last night before we even went in.

Plus, I constructed a little sales bonus for him using some other companies, in a very crafty manner, by utilizing an offshore brokerage firm where twenty percent accrues in a tax-free environment, which I can dispense into the cage at The Palms under his girlfriend's name.

Let him and his union buddies run amok.

I says, "Run amok Malik!"

What?

Packing?

You're kidding right?

The biggest players in the hemisphere are jettin' in so that you can potentially capture the flag.

Tell your wife tremors happen here every day.

Besides, no one will be able to fly in or out till tomorrow, due to the potential for more seismic activity and an ash cloud blowing in our direction.

That's right.

Rod, my Australian, called me just a half hour ago and says, "It don't look like we'll be able to get the sled up today, mate. Your islands are rockin' and startin' to spew. So it looks like we'll have to put our meeting off till tomorrow."

So I says to him, "No problem, 'cause Hassie and I have some business to iron out anyways, before we sit down and have our meeting with you."

And he was cool with that.

I mean, he's a best friend.

So tell the Mrs. to relax and enjoy the ride, 'cause she can't get off it anyways.

No, no.

The eruption isn't here.

There's no danger of that.

It's from one of the active volcanoes somewhere else in the chain.

I don't know which one, and does it really matter?

As long as it don't directly affect us, why should we care?

Anyway, this extra day will give us a chance to sit down and review some of my plans for your stock offering, 'cause however we structure it, there's gonna be potential for different degrees of quality.

Like caviar.

And it's gonna be our choice what we think will fit right, without it smelling badly.

Then we can get a menu going — good, better, best.

Like door one, two, or three — and you can pick.

You what?

You don't know if you want to pick anything?

Listen, bring the kid back to the guesthouse.

I'll get the wife, so Aseelah can see the fishies before the ash cloud rolls in. Then you and I will sit down, informally, and have a meeting, 'cause even if you do nothing, I still want to keep you as an intermediary, for other reasons. No matter what, we just have to make sure your project doesn't run amok, which it could, as exemplified by the fact that Aqua Venture came to me from two other sources all over the lot.

What I mean is, long before I bumped into you in Sydney, your deal got shown to me by some jerk-off outfit. They showed me the deal, and they wanted to borrow money on the stock — which was illiquid as cement — which is fine, because why would a guy come to me unless he had a problem.

Who are we? Goldman Sachs?

So it was shown to me by a broken down valise of a Florida promoter, who, for lack of a better word, is only used by firms — how can we say this politely — that are in need of a little oxygen. And let's face it, with your current burn rate, and those bridge loans comin' due, if you don't make a deal with me, there ain't gonna be any more lifeboats out there to pick up the slack.

Oh, you didn't think I knew about that little problem, did ya?

Well I do, so you can stop playin' it like, "Woo, woo, my shit don't stink. "

'Cause you're comin' to me on life support, and I'm trying to throw you a lifeline 'cause Morgan Stanley ain't touching this particular endeavor, and neither is anyone else, without a little creative flourishment.

That's where I come in.

We need to create interest and increase the float on your stock. Which, by the way, I have personally put some gas to, just to see how much buying power we need to apply in order to skin this cat.

I didn't tell you this yet, it's sort of a surprise...but I bought a few thousand shares just before the close on Friday. And we got a nice little spike going.

Check out the numbers.

I got it up one and three quarters with my puny buy order.

When a stock is so illiquid that it froths from five to seven dollars on three thousand shares, I know how to strategize, and trade the shit out of it. The only question is, which strategies we choose to bring the public to the plate, so that your little Bulletin Board stock, which, from what I can see, trades once a week by appointment only on a friends and family basis, can become a more globally traded issue.

So I gave it a little boost and it spiked nicely, which tells me that, as was told to me directly by my Aussie Rod with regard to cat-skinning strategy, "We need to construct a beaut — with great financial sophistication, that looks like a gilt-edge deal. Then we got an open door to create some real liquidity."

```
TO: Atlanta Jihad File
FROM: Patrick Fitzpatrick
Cc: AUSA Christopher Prim, Chief Securities Fraud Unit
AUSA David Hasty, Chief International Terrorism Unit
DATE: June 19, 2006
RE: Instructions to CW1
```

On June 19, 2006, I learned from Special Agent Kevin Farrow that CW1 had purchased approximately 3,000 shares of Aqua Venture (AVEN) in an open market transaction late in the day on Friday, June 16th. I had understood from Agent Farrow that he was pressured into buying the stock by subject, Jamal Hassim.

In a telephone debriefing later this morning, CW1 informed me that it was his idea to buy the stock to create market support. His rationale was to keep Jamal Hassim satisfied with the AVEN deal so that further discussions about union investment in Aqua Venture would be possible. He also noted that Jamal Hassim has plans to use the proceeds from fraudulent investments in AVEN stock to further global terrorism. Because of this potential threat to national security, CW1 stated that he felt he had no choice, and bought the stock in a series of transactions over several hours.

I then reiterated prior instructions not to engage in open market transactions. On prior occasions, I had explained to him that open market transactions are prohibited because they potentially disadvantage public investors. I further explained that the only potential exception to the bar on open market transactions is a situation where a subject instructs him to execute a trade and refusal to do so would tend to reveal his cooperation with the government.

I told CW1 not to sell the AVEN stock, reminded him again that there is a strict prohibition against his engaging in market transactions of any nature unless cleared by this office, and to await further instructions.

Special Agent Kevin Farrow and AUSA Jason Varlet participated in this morning's telephone call.

Tape 4B 6/19/2006
Side A begins

[REDACTED]

It reached $^3/_4$ and closed $2\,^{21}/_{32}$.

Not bad for a little stock, and just again to conclude the matter, I just spoke to the company and they had two meetings.

One was with Wal-Mart and the other with Bergen Brunswick.

It should have gone very well and hopefully we'll be reading about it.

I'm going to conference you in with Rodney Flitch in Australia.

I'm gonna provide a little detail on how you're a friendly guy.

Jot down this number.

His daily number in Australia is 011 612 9253 8200.

Correct.

That's Rodney Flitch, chairman of the biggest insurance company in Australia.

We're gonna do it right now.

Here's my game plan before we get on the phone. I'm going to get on the phone, I'm going to prep him, then I'm gonna be zero locked out.

I'm gonna say, Norton this, Rodney this, Norton this. I'm going to chat for a few minutes, then what you're going to do is you guys will take it from there. I'll ring off, and you call him back directly, and you two guys just do what you need to do together. I'll make sure everything stays right down center lane.

No, I really want you to have a direct dialogue with Rodney. If this thing works you two guys are friends for life.

And you're dealing with your counterpart only with a little more latitude, because he's in a less restricted part of the world, so I'm going to put you on hold and conference him in.

Norton? You still there?

I don't know what happened.

He got called out.

We'll try again later, but before I ring off, are you in front of your screen?

Good. Just give me a few quotes.

That's unbelievable!

ECCS closed at $11^5/_{16}$?

When we started working that stock on Friday it was nine bucks!

That's a nice payday for me.

How about EACT? Another nine-dollar stock.

What's that?

Up $1^3/_4$ today?

Well, I wouldn't call it a spike, but we're starting to climb the Himalayas.

We've got a lot of volume set to come in on Thursday and Friday. This is gonna be hotter than a fuckin' firecracker, so you might want to load up on a little more.

This sector is hot anyway, but let's just make sure we don't move it too fast.

The chart needs to be a five day-er so it don't look too goofy.

Malik, Malik? Is that you skulking around?

Hold on.

Let me just hang up the phone.

Norton, I'll speak to you later, buddy.

Hey, Malik, who let you in?

She was supposed to leave a half hour ago!

Well, I'm glad to hear she's gone now, anyways.

I had to get Jamal's wife outta here. She's mucking up the works.

She's always skulking around the guesthouse givin' me the evil eye.

And thanks to her, now I gotta deal with Candy running around talking like Bono.

Can you imagine?

Candy!

Repeatin' all kinds of communist help-the-less-fortunate crap.

To which I says, "Put your head back in the bag and have another gimlet."

Which, thank God, she's only too happy to do — her being Candy.

But still, who wants to be dealing with that?

[RESUME]

I'll tell ya, I don't know how Hassie takes it, having to listen to that happy horseshit all the time. If it were me, I'd fuckin' lose my mind.

I mean, I understand about creating a smoke screen, but what she does is over the line.

That's why I like dealing with him, 'cause he's straight up about his intentions. He just wants support for the stock, so after we juice it, he can sell most of it back.

Oh, don't be stupid.

Of course, he ain't gonna come right out and say it.

And part of it is personality.

He's quiet from all those years taking orders, like most of them military types.

But make no mistake, he wants to be under the exit before the whole thing collapses.

Stevie Wonder could see it, it's so obvious.

On this I know I'm right.

What's that?

You don't think what?

He won't do anything illegal?

Have you completely lost your mind?

Listen, we're very clever at what we're doing.

He knows exactly what we're up to.

We're not sticking up banks at gunpoint here.

We're a bunch of slippery eels.

We know what we're doing and we'll cover up the tracks nicely.

The key to all this stuff is deniability. You can't do something stupid with no deniability.

Don't tell me he don't know that.

He ain't no one's fool.

He went to the Air Force Academy for God's sakes, which means he's got a hell of a lot more intellectual firepower than you — and you know what's going on.

So don't tell me he doesn't know exactly what the deal is.

Make no mistake.

He's down for the game.

A loan?

How big a marker do you have this time?

I'll tell you what, I'll give you the two grand, not as a loan, but as a down payment on a project that I...excuse me, *we* need to accomplish.

That's right, we.

Before you leave you're gonna take these Aqua Venture promo packages to pass on to your friends.

You know, those friends I was telling Hassie about last night.

I know, I know.

I got a little carried away.

But I do believe that you could have a potential earn here with Hassim's stock if we play our cards right.

If you get some of your detectives involved I'll throw you commission and a few shares for free.

We need to generate a little excitement here, and let Jiminy think that we're conferencing with these characters so I can set the table, and get him to let me put his stock in play — which will create the potential to make this a very profitable transaction at the end of the day.

[REDACTED]

So what if there's no meetings yet?

We'll have one with your detective friends telephonically fairly quickly, and we'll have other unions that could be interested — or almost interested — in a few days.

So take these and send them out to your bent nose buddies. You know, those ones that are friends with the Lucheses at Local 138.

And your friend Ralphie at the Operating Engineers — that's an excellent idea.

Send one to him, then we'll follow it up with a call, like, "Hey, why don't you pass this on to certain cousins."

See if they want to participate.

The point being, we have to be able to say we sent 'em a FedEx with some semblance of the plan. If it looks like we have some firepower and influence I can dangle the rib roast, and get Hassie on board with the stock deal I've constructed for Aqua Venture, which he won't want to turn down if he thinks there's five hundred million on the plate.

He can't. He can't.

[RESUME]

So send these out to your friends, like that skipper from the Gambinos your cousin used to hang with on Mulberry Street.

Yeah, yeah.

And those wise guys at Local 136. Send it to them too.

It don't matter if we get a decision, or a second call, in three weeks or two.

The point being, even if it's just a telephone meeting, let's just say, "Hello, this is Jamal Hassim, this is my cousin Ralph, this is my friend Ed."

I just need to wave a big pork chop so I can do what I want, which you can help me accomplish with a few little "how do you do's."

FEDERAL BUREAU OF INVESTIGATION

Date of transcription 6/19/06

Source, who is in a position to testify, provided the following information:

During the course of a debriefing on June 19, 2006, source advised he was incorrect when he stated that NORTON MERRICK controls 80% of Merrico Book Club (MBAC). Rather, source has learned that Merrick controls only 8% of MBAC's stock, and recalled that his initial information about the size of Merrick's stock position came from an individual named RICHIE GALLO, a broker at J.R. BARCLAY. Source now believes Gallo was "puffing" about Merrick so that he could entice source to provide "consulting work" for the publicly traded company DREMERT (stock symbol DRME). In exchange Gallo would give source 325,000 shares of DRME stock. It was unclear what type of consulting services the company was looking for the source to provide.

Source advised that MELVIN SMALLS (also known as MALIK EL-TIBERIUS) has indicated he will contact his associates from the LUCHESE and GAMBINO crime families about the AQUA VENTURE deal. Source believes Smalls is an AL QAEDA sympathizer, and advised that Smalls has already made contact with corrupt union officials from various New York unions, such as the DETECTIVES ENDOWMENT ASSOCIATION, the WESTCHESTER OPERATING ENGINEERS (LOCAL 138) and the NEW YORK PRODUCTION WORKERS (LOCAL 136) about the possible purchase of AQUA VENTURE stock.

Investigation on 6/19/06 at New York, New York (telephonically)

File # 196C — NY-236083

By SA Kevin Farrow   Date dictated 6/19/06

Tape 4C 6/19/2006
Side A

Good news! The boat is back in the harbor, and the girls are great.

Candy says they'll have to stay downtown overnight, though; the ash fall bein' too thick for driving home safe.

So I says to her, "Buy the kid some lunch at the Palms, then go and take a load off at the spa."

She says, "No problem. Tell Jamal Ahn and Aseelah are in the very best hands."

So take a seat and enjoy some lunch.

I'll catch you up with our plans.

Mingo, I said no pork!

I specifically says to him, "*Blakman blong Amerika no kakae pig*," and you see what happens? Pork chops from Chief Tanna!

They are good, I've gotta say.

And we know they're fresh!

It's a good thing Mingo boiled up some coconut crab too. The garlic sauce they're in is one of his specialties.

Coconut crabs are the largest land crabs in the world.

The one you're eating now was probably forty years old before Mingo grabbed it, bagged it, and stuck it in a thermal spring.

These crabs hang out mostly around my palm trees, eating my harvest. I tell Mingo, "Kill all those fuckers, I don't give a shit if they're almost extinct."

There are some creatures that don't deserve to live, them being some of them. So I've declared a kind of jihad on them.

Mingo has carte blanche to kill them by any means necessary.

I don't care how he does it as long as they're dead, and served up on a platter.

Oh, don't get all misty-eyed.

This one's cooked already, so we might as well pick the carcass.

Have another leg. Let Mingo crack the nippers.

Candy loves these things.

Believe it or not, she was a model in the seventies.

I keep telling her, if she doesn't put down the fork, even them muumuus ain't gonna fit anymore, and what does she do?

She just gives me a dirty look and has Mingo split another claw.

We may not be able to control these women, but at least we can make sure they don't control us. What do they know anyways?

Alls they do is spend our money, but they got no idea how to earn.

Oh, no. I didn't notice that, about Ahn bein' a bioengineer.

I looked at the math, not the marketing.

Even so, with all her fancy degrees, what will she make in the open market?

Fifty, sixty grand?

I don't know about you, but that won't even cover the monthly balance on my American Express.

My point is, Malik ran up to collect all your promo packs just about an hour ago, and he says, "It's a foregone conclusion with the unions."

Like, it's for sure you're gonna get passed.

No, no. I'm not kiddin'.

All these union guys are great friends of ours.

The deck is stacked on this.

Malik's got connections all over the New York area with certain cousins, like at Local 138 — those are Operating Engineers — and 136 — the Production Workers — which is a little bit of a bent-nose outfit where we're very friendly with the business manager, Johnny Z.

Johnny Z.'s predecessor just recently got a case of lead poisoning, so Johnny's in control now.

That's a good question — I don't know how he got it, as in, I'm not sure how many pieces of lead poisoned him. But he's gone, and now Johnny's our go-to guy.

So Johnny's gonna get your package tomorrow and he says that as soon as he does that he'll pass it to the inspector general so we can potentially get approval within the next few weeks. And that's a billion dollar fund right there.

Then there's the Detectives Endowment Association, which is about sixty million, and it looks like we're buzzing in there on the tenth of next month. The president of that union is Malik's former neighbor in Queens. So Malik and I have already had a meeting, telephonically, with him, and he says, "I like it. It looks so good. I want you to present this at the next board meeting so we can vote on it for approval."

So now that we know the unions are in the bag, we need to put our heads together and come up with a retail plan that will pass the smell test.

I'd be happy to hear your marketing ideas.

And yes —

Of course, you'll participate in the presentation we make next month to the detective boys.

Without a doubt.

See, the way I see your deal is this. I think of it as a big game of musical chairs, and if we're smart enough to have the chair when the music stops, then we'll be in good shape, since we'll be all cashed out when everything collapses, and then we go back and pick up the pieces.

'Cause he who has the cash wins.

When you say to make nothing — there's no reason to make nothing.

And no, breaking even ain't an option.

No one is going to fund you from the goodness of their hearts, this is what I've been spending the last few days trying to get you to understand.

That's why when I first saw your deal on an independent basis — and it's peculiar because it was basically shown to me from two sources that I didn't consider credible — and forgot it. But I gave it a quick once over, and even though I found it fascinating, I initially took a pass, because I knew — all good intentions aside — the only thing any of my investors are gonna ask about is, "What's in it for me?"

See, we like to take significant portions of companies, anywhere ranging from ten to twenty million with our own money, okay, to give ourselves an advantage. And if it gets larger than that, which Aqua Venture potentially will, we tend to bring in the Rolodex that says, "Break glass when needed."

That's what will arrive here tomorrow, if the ash cloud dissipates in time.

What?

At the window?

Chief Tanna! Stop pounding! *Yu stap toktok krangle olsem wanem?*

Kam in. Wanem rong?

His problem?

Well, besides being only two generations more advanced than Java man, he's afraid of devils.

What can you expect from a man who still makes fire from rubbing wood?

I'll tell ya why he's afraid.

It's because he thinks there's someone about to die.

See, I'm the local *nakaimo*.

Every island has one.

It's my job to supervise the bad spirits and keep them under control, which, surprisingly enough, comes very naturally to me.

I know, it's hard to imagine that anyone would think a skulky little stockbroker with a receding hairline could have power over life and death — but that's my reputation in this part of the world.

What's got his bowels in an uproar today is this ash storm.

The Nambas believe volcanoes breathe, and that a person's spirit gets sucked into a volcanic crater at the moment of death.

And you could understand why these nincompoops would think that.

The vents up there suck in oxygen and exhale cinder. In and out, in and out...until enough pressure builds beneath the surface and they blow.

Kaboom!

There ain't no appeals, and no second chances.

One spew of brimstone, and everything gets wiped away.

That's the world that the Nambas live in, so we gotta forgive them for their little superstitions.

We all got them.

Like when I owned a broker-dealer downtown and I was getting ready to cull the herd to make a big move on a stock, I would shave my mustache for luck.

When I walked into the office with a clean face — that's when my brokers knew it was time to make a push.

Oh, no, no, no.

We treated everything carefully, professional-like, so as not to set off any bells and whistles. And we represented a lot of bully stocks, like yours, that had a good story line but not a lot of steam.

Listen, not for nothing, right now Aqua Venture is a debt instrument involving a piece of land and some fishing rights in a broke-down third-world country with Al Qaeda training camps hidden in the jungles.

Well, you can argue all day long that there are no Talabanies in the mountains, and that all the press about the southern Philippine islands becoming the new training center for Jemaah Islamiyah and other terrorist groups is nothing but a ploy by Manila to use U.S. military support to help wipe out Muslim separatists only lookin' for independence, but that's not the perception that's been created.

Life is a perception game.

Who's to say what's real?

And furthermore, who cares, as long as we profit on the deal.

Voila!

A new bowl of kava!

Let's drink to health, wealth, and Aqua Venture, up three dollars in six weeks, closing at eight!

Hey, Mingo!

Tell your *bigman* the *bigfala* says no one's getting sucked into the volcano today.

And tell him this...tell him that when it does blow, he ain't gonna be the one goin' down.

SOUTHERN DISTRICT OF NEW YORK
UNITED STATES OF AMERICA
v.
MELVIN SMALLS (A/K/A MALIK EL-TIBERIUS),
JAMAL HASSIM (A/K/A "JIMMY" HASSIM), and
AHN HASSIM,

      Defendants.

     UNITED STATES COURTHOUSE
     40 FOLEY SQUARE
     NEW YORK, NEW YORK

     June 19, 2006
     10:17 am

APPEARANCES: PATRICK FITZPATRICK, ESQ.
     Assistant United States District Attorney

     DANA J. DEFAULT
     Acting Court Reporter

(Witness enters room.)

KEVIN FARROW, called as a witness, having been duly sworn by Judge Grayling, testified as follows:

THE WITNESS: Yes, I do.

BY MR. FITZPATRICK:

 Agent Farrow, this is continued emergency testimony concerning Aqua Venture, Melvin Smalls, Jamal Hassim, and Ahn Hassim. Let it be duly noted that the government has requested that this hearing be conducted in secret, as the information to be presented before this court may have national security implications.

Q. You testified two days ago concerning a scheme to defraud and support terrorism, and I am going to ask you two sets of questions about additional pieces of evidence that have come to our attention since you last testified.

First, what I want to ask you about is a conversation that occurred on or about June 19th of this year between the confidential witness, Mr. Skilling, and Jamal Hassim. Are you aware of such a conversation?

A. Yes.

Q. Have you been apprised about a tape recording of it?

A. Yes I have.

Q. By whom?

A. Conner Skilling, an FBI informant.

Q. Where were Mr. Skilling, Mr. Hassim, and Mr. Smalls when this recording was made?

A. They were at a restaurant on the island of Efate, in Melanesia, called Rossi's.

Q. And can you summarize for the court the substance of that recording?

A. Yes. Mr. Smalls and Mr. Hassim discussed wanting to start a fraudulent scheme to pay off union officials at the Detectives Endowment Association, Local 138 — the Westchester Operating Engineers, and Local 136 — the New York Production Workers, by paying bribes to corrupt union officials in order to encourage investment in Aqua Venture, Mr. Hassim's company.

Q. Where is this bribe money to come from?

A. A kickback offered to Mr. Skilling by Mr. Hassim for placing investors in his fraudulent scheme.

Q. We'll get to the planned terrorism connected to this scheme in a minute, but first I'd like to ask you if there is anything unusual about the union leadership of Local 136?

A. Yes. The New York Production Workers Local 136 is controlled by John Zambroni. He's a made man with the Gambino crime family.

Q. And how did Mr. Zambroni come to be in this position?

A. His predecessor, Randall Smalls, Melvin Smalls' cousin, disappeared approximately six months ago. The FBI believes he was murdered.

Q. Now to the second portion of our questioning. What has Conner Skilling told you about the intentions behind the establishment of the Aqua Venture scheme?

A. It has been represented to Mr. Skilling that Aqua Venture is a "front" established to provide monetary and technical support for Islamic militants training in the mountains of Mindanao, Sulu, and other Muslim islands in the southern Philippines. These islands have a long history of terrorist activity. It has been brought to the attention of the FBI and other U.S. authorities that Jemaah Islamiyah, the terrorist group that was responsible for the 2002 night club bombing in Bali that killed more than two hundred people, is drawing recruits from a number of countries, including Indonesia, Malaysia, Pakistan, and the Middle East to its mountain training camps in the southern Philippines, mostly on the island of Mindanao. Basically, this is a shift in operations now that we've shut down the Qaeda training camps in Afghanistan. The FBI believes that the training camps in Mindanao are under the control of the Moro Islamic Liberation Front, which has been engaged in a guerilla war for an independent state for twenty-five years. Aqua Venture

claims that its objective is to offer Moro separatists the economic
security they currently lack through the development of commercial
fish farms off the coast of Mindanao in an effort to persuade them to
put down their arms. We believe, based on recorded statements
made by Mr. Hassim to Mr. Smalls and Mr. Skilling, that the real
intention behind the Aqua Venture scheme is to develop, train, and
support international terrorists.

Q. Is there a specific statement attributable to Mr. Hassim that
you can share with the court that will make this more clear?

A. Yes. On June 17, 2006, Jamal Hassim stated to Mr. Skilling
and Mr. Smalls, and I quote, "There are over a hundred war passages in the Koran that one could say call for holy war, or jihad,
against unbelievers. I believe in Ayatollah Khomeini's interpretation, which states it is the Muslim duty to defend Muslim interests
against the Great Satan by all means possible. Mohammad said, 'Let
there be no hostility except to those who practice oppression.' In my
opinion Western policy has been consistently oppressive toward the
Muslim community since the days of Saladin, which entitles
Muslims, under Koranic law, to retaliate with whatever methods and
weapons are available to them."

Q. Has it also come to your attention that Mr. Hassim may be
trying to conceal his real identity in order to gain access to sensitive
information that may compromise national security?

A. There are many reasons to be concerned about Jamal
Hassim and the security threat he poses. He is an air force major,
currently serving in the Reserves, with intimate, in-depth knowledge
of military bases, storage depots, and advanced weaponry, including
our most sophisticated fighter jets. In addition, he has recently
requested a counterfeit detective's badge from Melvin Smalls, a corrupt former detective with the Manhattan vice squad, who is a
known Islamic militant and terrorist sympathizer. Our source also

tells us that Jamal Hassim has recently taken on an alias.

Q. Has Jamal Hassim engaged in other covert activities that indicate that he has intentions of using the proceeds from Aqua Venture illicitly?

A. Yes. Jamal Hassim has recently requested that our informant, Mr. Skilling, assist him in creating a phony offshore company, into which he plans to place his illegal earnings from Aqua Venture. It is intended to be a terrorist slush fund, from which money can be dispensed secretly, without Federal scrutiny, to mujahedeen in the Philippines, Indonesia, Pakistan, and beyond.

Q. Has the FBI identified any other members of this conspiracy?

A. We have. Wiretaps of clandestine conversations Mr. Hassim has been conducting from Conner Skilling's guesthouse phone line have helped us to identify other terrorist leaders involved in this plot.

Q. Are there any other "key players" you have been able to identify that you can tell the grand jury about today?

A. This is a far-reaching conspiracy with many participants, some of whom are still in the process of being identified. Because of the highly sensitive nature of this investigation I am not at liberty to disclose any additional names at this time. What I can say is there is one suspect in particular who has given us great cause for concern. He is the spiritual leader, or imam, of Jamal Hassim's mosque, and appears to be a central figure in this scheme. For purposes of national security, I am only allowed to identify this individual as "Senior Al Qaeda Suspect Number One" at this time.

Q. Is there an identifiable pattern of behavior that indicates this individual poses a high-level threat to national security?

A. Yes. Intercepted phone calls between Jamal Hassim and "Senior Al Qaeda Suspect Number One," appear to be conducted in code. FBI analysts believe that illegal money transfers and planned bio-terror attacks are discussed between these two suspects in terms of types of seaweed and species of fish.

Q. Is there any new information about Ahn Hassim that the FBI has recently learned about which poses a potential risk to homeland security?

A. Yes. It has been recently discovered that Ahn Hassim, a Philippine national from Mindanao, has an advanced degree in bio-engineering from MIT. The FBI is currently investigating her employment at the Centers for Disease Control, and believes she intends to use her scientific expertise to assist the Moro Liberation Front in staging a devastating bio-terrorism attack against the U.S.

FROM: CW1
SENT: Monday, June 19, 2006 2:40:16 PM
TO: Agent Farrow
Cc: Agent Lossman, AUSA Patrick Fitzpatrick, AUSA Jason Varlet
SUBJECT: Expansion plans

Greetings from Port Vila:

I hope all is well. As you know, it has been very busy out here. While Jamal Hassim is making clandestine phone calls on the other side of the house, I thought I'd duck into my office and give you a short summary of the planned events for today:

When Jamal returns I will have the blunt, breakaway conversation with him that we spoke about last night concerning proposed marketing strategies for AVEN, including:

1. Hiring promoters who bribe brokers as an inducement to sell stock with payouts of cash or stock sent to an offshore nominee name.

2. A pump and dump scheme whereby my investor group gets most of the free trading shares of AVEN cheaply or heavily discounted, inflates the price, then sells it off ahead of the market.

3. Stock "put away" by bribed brokers with "no net sales allowed."

4. A couple of market makers in AVEN stock who trade it back and forth to create a false appearance of liquidity and market demand.

5. The use of "cold calls" to solicit investment, made by unregistered brokers who falsely use the names of registered brokers who hold Series 7 registration.

After speaking to Mr. Fitzpatrick, I understand the importance of offering this same marketing approach for the Bangsamoro Seaweed Planters Association (BSPA), and will endeavor to do so in the same conversation. I will also make sure to probe Mr. Hassim on the subject of botulism, now that you have made me aware of his wife's research on this disease.

At the risk of sounding too patronizing, I want to thank you for your efforts to provide Candy and me with protection and backup support. I understand that the remoteness of our location slows down these efforts. We know we are likely dealing with very dangerous criminals here, and have taken as many precautions as we can to protect ourselves and the continuity of the ongoing investigation. Much more should be developing here rapidly. When it does, I'll send you PART 2.

Talk to you soon.

Tape 4D 6/19/06
Side B

You'll be happy to know that I finally talked Chief Tanna into clearing out of here.

It is pretty amazing.

But you know me, I never present ideas to people that they're gonna say no to.

They may have an objection, but that's only a temporary no.

He sure was resistant.

You're right.

But while you were on the phone, I came up with a plan.

I says to the chief, "Let's have a private conversation with the spirits out by my sacred tree."

So while you were busy checking on the wife, I got the chief out back, which is why you didn't see.

So I take him to this hole in the ground I outfitted with a hollow pole; and I start chanting, "*Fakof, fakof, fakof! Mi wantem se yu mas faof naoia nomo!*" Which basically means, "Get the fuck out of here if you know what's good for you!" And since I'm shoutin' into an underground tunnel, my voice starts echoing back...

"*Fakof, fakof, fakof!*"

So Tanna is convinced that he's witnessing a dialogue between me and some invisible spook.

And you know what happens next?

Right in the middle of this hubbub the ash thins out.

Whoosh!

It gets blown off by a breeze.

Chief Tanna is so delighted — 'cause he thinks this means the bad spirits are in retreat — that he hangs this boar's tusk around my neck, and scampers away lickity split back down to his village, mutterin' something about preparin' a feast.

Now, I don't claim to be entirely responsible, but it does look like visibility will improve tomorrow.

My buddy Rod and Sheik Abdullah are ready to fly in as soon as they can get clearance.

I was just on my radio, talking to people around the islands that are trackin' the storm — and they tell me the density peaked around an hour ago, which means that the girls should be able to drive back up from the hotel in the morning.

Listen, it's good they happened to be in town when the cloud hit anyways.

This way they don't have to be bored with our business plans, which we should start by takin' a seat, and tippin' back a couple more shells. And you can't say no, 'cause it will be an insult to Mingo, since he personally pounded the roots.

Oh, no, no, no.

The girls' hotel bill has already been taken care of.

It's on me. I insist.

I'm extremely close to people who run things on a personal level, so I get all kinds of special deals.

So what I'm looking for, what I basically wanna do, since we're friends, is to talk turkey and finish things up. The only thing left to decide, as I see it, is which way to structure it, so that we end up with an instrument whereby we accrue the largest aggregate chop.

What I mean is, there's a compendium of brainpower I bring to the table — and people who trust me to find products for them know that.

Like Malik, for instance.

He'll probably invest five million in Aqua Venture, and he has a couple of go-to guys, besides the union guys, which maybe, just out of proving he's part of the fraternity, he can introduce to the deal for a few million bucks.

And I think I mentioned before that Malik likes to promote stocks like Aqua Venture and your seaweed company.

So if we want to do a retail promotion on those stocks, Malik'll take care of the brokers the right way.

See, Malik and I have done some preliminary rooting around. We found only three market makers for Aqua Venture. And since it goes days without trading, it's almost completely illiquid.

Let's face it, if someone were to sell five thousand shares of Aqua Venture today, the price would drop five dollars.

You saw how easily I juiced it.

It spiked two dollars on a lousy three thousand share trade.

There are no legit Wall Street firms that are gonna support a company with a market cap of seventy million dollars, that trades like it's got cancer.

Well, I'm glad you agree.

These small cap stocks are hard to get jump-started, and sometimes they need a little resuscitation to get notoriety, after which they take on a life of their own.

It looks like you have a good management team, and if you can create some sustainable buying activity with an Internet promotion or something like that, you might have a good shot to use the stock as currency and make some deals, if you've got a clever CFO.

I have that same idea.

But between you and me, if you get out of one-point-three million shares of this at nine bucks or twelve bucks, enough!

And, if you want to play with your restricted shares after you get something going to maximize profitability, you can funnel your profit into a numbered account, with a backchannel to whatever fuckin' charity, help the mujahedeen organization you want.

Am I wrong about that?

What do you give a fuck?

I understand you don't want to kill the stock. And let's face it, we couldn't do that if we wanted to.

How can you kill something that's deader than Kelsey's nuts?

I don't argue that it may have some intrinsic value.

And some good stocks trade inefficiently.

You're right.

But how efficiently can any stock trade when it's basically controlled by a single shareholder?

I took a little peek at your shareholder base.

Not for nothin', but you own seventy-three percent of the controlling interest!

And who owns the rest?

Let me guess, people from your mosque, and some friends of the same religious persuasion?

That's what I thought.

You probably get a call on your cell phone before any of them are gonna make an appointment to put down a trade like, "This is your mullah calling, glory be to Allah, I bought a thousand shares today."

You don't even need to answer me on that one, 'cause I already know the answer.

You misconstrue what I'm sayin'.

I'm not trying to denigrate your company.

I understand you're trying to build it and make it work.

It always pays to do that, because at the end of the day, it has to have the appearance of something that actually does some business — as opposed — I mean, clearly you and I can invent four million shares off the lint of the couch in our basement, and have it trading in forty-five days — but at the end of the day it's going to zero.

Listen, I wanna do something with retail like I want three horns on my head. But let's not mince words, I'd rather be sitting here and creating AVEN, owning shares at twenty-five cents and having the stock at twelve in two months than begging for investment money at thirty dog and pony shows, which generate an interest level of next to nothing.

The point is, with so much of the float concentrated in so few hands, Aqua Venture is custom made for juicing.

This is why you're gonna need to transfer half of all your freely traded Aqua Venture shares into an offshore account controlled by me. As compensation, I figure you'll give me those shares for free, since they're almost worthless anyway.

You would never do that?

Then I'll have you sell me half of your stake for a nominal fee, say twenty-five cents a share, or something like that.

Wait, wait. Before you say anything else just let me finish — 'cause this is the important part.

See, after you sell me half your float, Malik and I will park it in a shell company controlled by one of our friends, like my very, very dear friend the sheik from Indonesia.

He has a shell company here in Vanuatu called Alchemy.

Once we roll the Aqua Venture shares into Alchemy, we'll open up a corporate account at Sheik Ali's bank in Java. We'll cross trade back and forth between Alchemy and Java National Bank to raise your profile and get some attention from the street.

When that's done, all we have to do is have Malik contact some of the brokerage houses he does business with back in the States, and make a deal with some friendly brokers to push the stock. Then we wire a stock certificate for two hundred thousand shares into some bullshit holding company at ANZ Bank.

The CEO of the brokerage firm, who, by the way, happens to be a personal friend, will draw on the shares in that account to pay off his brokers.

You have to understand, most of these kids, they're not Series 7, they're just knockaround guys who went to Bensonhurst High and like to hang around the video arcade after work. But make no mistake, this is a group of very, very highly trained professionals, and they know how to bullet a stock.

They tell me they think they can get Aqua Venture running up to twelve dollars in just forty-five days.

These are no jerk-offs.

They know how to put stock away.

Once they retail your stock to Mrs. Magilacutty, they ain't gonna let her sell it out into the open market again until after we've taken our profit, no matter how hard she screams. And if she threatens to make some kind of official complaint, then we make the brokers cross her stock off with another buyer, for a sale of the same size.

That's how we sustain the market.

We push it up, and it holds, we push it up, and it holds...until we determine it's time to take a profit, and then we make sure we're all cashed out before anyone else can make a move.

So now you have the full menu.

A. We're gonna do the brokerage deal.

B. We're gonna do the Internet deal.

Or C — We'll do both.

I suppose you could say no, but I don't think you'll be so inclined.

Malik's brokers are gonna give you a genuine turbo boost, and put Aqua Venture front and center, right in the heart of prime time.

There'll be press and analyst coverage.

If we can get this thing fired up fast enough, you might even get mentioned on CNBC.

Of course, we won't tell 'em your wife works with botulism 'cause that wouldn't be good for the storyline.

I'll tell you what, when it comes to that stuff you're a braver man than me.

I wouldn't want Candy near no poison, especially after I get the MasterCard bill, and I gotta get tough.

You never know what motivation lurks in people.

I mean, your wife could say, "I'm sick of having most of my money tied up in an aqua culture business that I can't get no one but my friends at the local mosque to invest in. Maybe I'll collect on the life insurance plan by slippin' some botulism from the lab storehouse into Jamal's soup," or something like that.

I know, I know.

It's highly regulated and only used for experiments.

I understand.

Alls I'm saying is, when you're dealin' with someone with that kind of deadly expertise, a higher potential for skullduggery exists. Though it has to be said, it's good to have her oversight and advice, what with botulism bein' common in fish.

Just don't tell that to any of your mujahedeen, whatever you do.

Or next thing you know they'll be poisoning our Star Kist!

Oh, don't get all offended.

I have a little quip for everything, as you know by now with me.

You're a CEO out of central casting, with a resume beyond impeccable, what with you flying fighter planes and your wife's background as a foreign research fellow at the CDC.

You guys are great headline material, with a story that's got good fizz.

Alls we need is to publish worldwide over the Internet through my dear friend from Indonesia, who owns a number of promotional sites overseas that you'll definitely want to use to publicize your seaweed and fish.

I'll tell ya something, if we get eighteen of his websites on this thing in one day the stock's gonna go to forty, and you know where we're gonna end up?

The food's not too good, although it's free.

So now you're gonna have to make a decision.

I told Malik and Ali, although I can't speak for you, "I'm sure Hassim's gonna want to sit down tomorrow with the both of you, after Ali arrives in town, and likely do the Internet and the brokerage together, in somewhat of a coordinated fashion so they complement each other. Maybe he can even create some news we can disseminate."

Oh, you already have a possible merger in the pipeline?

You're better at this than I thought!

Under these circumstances, what I would do if I were you is wire two hundred thousand shares of your fish and seaweed stock into Alchemy today.

What's the harm?

If you send them the shares and nothing happens in the next five or six days then you can put a stop transfer on it.

I know Malik's brokers are talking about getting the stock delivered tomorrow so they can fit you into their time scheme.

You want to contemplate?

Fine.

But just remember one thing. Your current business model isn't working.

In order for me to generate any interest with my investors, I'm gonna have to be able to tell them that you're trying new and more aggressive marketing plans.

The point being, before my Aussie and my Indonesian sit down for our power lunch you're gonna have to tell me if you're gonna fish or cut bait.

This is the point of no return for me.

So tomorrow is the pivotal day in determining what we do.

The only question is, how are we going to do it?

From: CW1
Sent: Monday, June 19, 2006 4:00:37 PM
To: Agent Farrow
Cc: Agent Lossman, AUSA Patrick Fitzpatrick, AUSA Jason Varlet
Subject: PART 2

Greetings from Port Vila:

The following will serve to confirm the continuing events of 6/19/06 as they have unfolded thus far.

All of the marketing plans we discussed for Aqua Venture and
Bangsamoro Seaweed were presented to Mr. Hassim in great detail when
he returned to my living room after making a series of secret phone calls.
The discussions were very detailed about the desired price movements,
manipulations, and liquidity on these deals. He has expressed interest in
of all of the proposed endeavors, including:

1. Methodology of brokerage promotions, including cross trades, "put
   away" stock, bribing brokers and the creation of offshore accounts
   for bribes and illegal kickbacks.

2. The need for the promotion to be coordinated with phony news
   stories.

3. The use of fraudulent Internet promotions to augment the news
   cycle, and illegal brokerage methods.

Hassim is currently back at the guesthouse deciding which of the proposed plans to use to "get things going," and when to start their imple-
mentation. Though we haven't come to a final resolution on the extent of
my compensation, Mr. Hassim indicated to me that he would likely be
willing to sell me half the float of Aqua Venture for 25 cents a share, and
convert his restricted shares into freely traded stock. Furthermore, he
has unequivocally confirmed that Aqua Venture stock is held almost
exclusively by a small group of radical Muslims that belong to his mosque
who regularly engage in insider trading, by tipping each other off before a
stock purchase in AVEN is made. He further revealed that he plans to
bank his illegal profits from the brokerage scheme in an offshore entity
called Alchemy, then transfer these funds to terrorist organizations overseas.

Security Commentary:

The information I shared with you on the phone about Ahn Hassim, and her access to large quantities of liquid botulism, is incredibly specific. Be very careful at this point what "stones are turned over." She is very dangerous, and possibly alert to my role. For this reason I have tried to limit my association with her. I know you are widening your investigation into the Hassim's personal and professional affairs stateside. I must caution you to be as discreet as possible because of the violent nature of our targets, and their access to weapons of mass destruction. We must continue to be vigilant, especially now, on security matters.

SECRET ORCON
ALL INDIVIDUALS HANDLING THIS INFORMATION ARE REQUIRED TO
PROTECT IT FROM UNAUTHORIZED DISCLOSURE IN THE INTEREST OF
THE NATIONAL SECURITY OF THE UNITED STATES

PERTINENT EVIDENCE INVENTORY
Agency Case Number 3252
19 June 2006
Index of Relevant Government Exhibits
Evidence gathered from the FBI search of property domiciled at 1031 Donnybrook Ave, Atlanta, Georgia, approved June 19, 2006, by Secret Intelligence Court Judge William S. Grayling, in furtherance of the sealed intelligence investigation of Jamal M. Hassim and Ahn H. Hassim, pursuant to charges of supporting international terrorism, counseling others to wage war against the United States, aiding and abetting enemy combatants, wire fraud, mail fraud, conspiracy to commit securities fraud, conspiracy to commit bribery,

conspiracy to use biological weapons in furtherance of violent crime, membership in known terrorist organizations and espionage:

1. Thirty (30) Cipro capsules, 500 mg each
2. Two one hundred dollar bills not sequentially numbered
3. Various wrist bands, day passes, brochures and park maps from Wet n' Wild, Orlando, Florida; Splash n' Safari, Santa Claus, Indiana; Noah's Ark, Wisconsin Dells, Wisconsin; Raging Waters, San Dimas, California; Gilligan's Island Water Theme Park, Hope, New Jersey; Wet n' Wild, Las Vegas, Nevada
4. Season pass, Six Flags White Water Park, Marietta, Georgia
5. Various video tapes and photographs of high profile water rides including but not limited to "Dragon's Den," "Dark Voyage," and "Run Away River"
6. Two (2) copies of Poor Richard's Almanac (2004 and 2005)
7. One Rand McNally World Globe
8. Road maps for New York, California, Wisconsin, New Jersey, and Indiana
9. Air Force dress blues
10. Various Air Force medals including Longevity, Northern Watch, Southern Watch, Aerial Achievement, Commendation, Meritorious Service, and Distinguished Flying Cross
11. Kuwaiti Freedom Ribbon
12. War on Terrorism Ribbon
13. Green Air Force flight suit
14. Desert flight suit

15. Flight jacket

16. One Air Force Pistol (9mm)

17. Special Air Mission (SAM FOX) Air Force ID and badge issued to Major Jamal M. Hassim

18. Secret Security Clearance Line Badge, issued to Major Jamal M. Hassim

19. Photos of various national and international Air Force bases, including Pago Pago, Alice Springs, Australia; Grand Forks, North Dakota, and Minot, North Dakota

20. Exterior aerial photos of various U.S. fighter planes, including F-16, F-15, F-15E, F-111, B-52, B-1, B-2, AL-130, and F-22

21. Photos of various U.S. transport planes including the KC-135 air refueling tanker and C-17 transport

22. Interior photos of the Military Air Mission hangar at Andrews Air Force base, including pictures of VC-20A, VC-20H, VC-37A, C-40B, C-3A, and VC-9 jets utilized by the Special Air Mission (SAM FOX) Air Wing

23. Exterior ramp photos of Air Force One and Air Force Two

24. One Controlled Access badge for the Coordinating Center for Infectious Diseases, Food Borne Disease Division, Botulism Branch, issued to Dr. Ahn Hassim from the Centers for Disease Control, Atlanta

25. Two pairs of men's boxer shorts with the molecular structure of botulism bacteria pictured on the seat

26. One 32 oz container of Dannon low fat vanilla yogurt

27. One box of Presidential M&M's with the Presidential Seal

28. One (1) Hasbro Laser tag 2-Player Deluxe Set

29. Two (2) Hasbro Laser tag Team Comm Headsets

Tape 4E 6/19/06
Side B continues

[REDACTED]

Hi genius!

You're a little early.

I'm assuming you brought your friend from the naka-mal, and that he knows his new name.

So he's got it then, Sheik Abdullah Ali; Trade Minister from Indonesia, a fund manager with three hundred million...he does this, he does that.

Basically, he does whatever I say he does.

Make sure you tell him that he comes from Java, where he just bought a bank — and Jamal Hassim is the aquaculture entrepreneur he never had.

What was that?

He says it'll cost me another fifty bucks if I want him to put the robes in play?

Tell your little kava clerk I know all there is to know about "play."

I play off everything. I'll play off the oil you use in the fryer.

I have no shame, I have no shame.

So tell your little Indian if he don't take my deal he can go back to that hut he pours for, where he can make less than half of what I'm offering in tips.

You go back and tell him that.

And tell him this too —

Tell him this will be the most insightful two hours he's ever spent.

I'm the smartest guy he'll ever meet.

There's more than two hundred dollars on the line here.

I'll teach him how not to pay rent.

[RESUME]

Mr. Hassim!

Welcome back.

I know this is short notice, but when my very, very dear friend and colleague Sheik Ali got clearance to land, he wanted to fly over this evening, ahead of Rod who's likely coming here tomorrow.

So when Ali says to me, "Conner, now that the dust has settled, I want to come right away," I says, "Great! Rod's already seen Jamal's presentation in Sydney and is ready to commit probably ten million, so he doesn't need to hear the pitch again."

And Ali says — correct me if I'm wrong — Ali says, "Tell Mr. Hassim that I'd like to see the Cliff Notes version of his business plan without getting into ultra detail, 'cause I've already done my due diligence on his company and I feel it's extremely undervalued because it's not distributed widely enough in public hands, which I can easily correct by publicizing it on all my South Asian websites in Indonesia and Malaysia and whatnot. These are the websites I use to raise millions of dollars for Muslim charities, and promote my own businesses, so it's no problem adding information about Aqua Venture, since the infrastructure is already there."

So I told my colleague here that I'd tell you to take yourself out of pitch mode, because he's already pre-sold...but he got here so fast that I didn't even have a chance to tell you before he showed up in my living room, which is why I'm telling you now.

I don't think I'm sayin' anything that's not correct when I say Ali's a very sophisticated investor, and as I told you before, he's the Trade Minister of Indonesia, and just closed on a bank in Java, where we can open a corporate account.

Ali also carries a diplomatic pouch, so if we need anything delivered, he's our man.

So, the way I see it, we have what I like to call a pre-tenderized situation, meaning that we're all predisposed to do business together, which means we don't have to hash over all the finer details.

These meetings are all the same, anyway. I know how it's gonna go already.

Everybody's gonna be bullshitting about how big a swinging dick they are, and how legitimate they are and all this other happy horseshit.

Ali's used to that, so he doesn't need a sell job, 'cause a re-hash will actually bore him.

So Malik will pour us each a shell, and then my very near and dear friend Jamal will give us a brief overview of his business plan.

A very, very brief one, which he'll confine to essentially a nice simple get-to-know-you chat — more kissy-face than an actual presentation — since we're all friends, and favorably inclined.

Then we'll get down to brass tacks and decide how we're going to achieve more retail buying, more shareholders, and more liquidity on the stock.

Because I'll tell you what, if our hands were sandpaper and our dicks were wood they'd be toothpicks by now.

We've been workin' this deal for the last four days.

I don't know about you, but I'm tired of jerkin' off.

So raise your shells, boys, and lets make a toast to sinking the

Aqua Venture deal tonight!

Hey, Jimmy —

Just so you know, I already hit Sheik Ali with a sort of preemptive strike.

I told him about the Air Force Academy and the re-fueling tankers, and the C-17 transports.

Which, by the way, Jimmy still flies as a member of the Reserves.

I like to joke — and I say this affectionately — that my new and dear friend is a walking intelligence failure.

I mean, not for nothin', but how do you take a kid out of the Robert Taylor Homes with SATs barely above the triple digits and train him to fly fighter jets, even if you accept him on probation and make him do an extra year in prep school?

I know, know.

Hassie is always reminding me that he never flew fighter jets, only transports. And he's always waving the flag. Like, "What a great country, giving a poor kid like me a chance. I just want to give back to the community. I want to eradicate poverty and injustice. Trade rakes for rockets. Fish for fighting. Pay them more than fifty cents a day. Show them that we aren't always favoring the Christian majority." World Bank, USAID, LEAP and all of that gobbledygook.

That's what he says.

Meanwhile he's married to Dr. Strangelove, cooking up bacterias in some back room, and giving job opportunities to members of Abu Syyaf, which I know Ali don't have any issue with, them being all over Indonesia and all.

But Hassie here, he's always playing patriot saying, "Oh golly, most of the mujahedeen on Mindanao are separatists, not terrorists, and if you provide them with development initiatives they're less likely to become dangerous or remain a threat. Alls they want is economic equality. Over twenty-four thousand former combatants already reintegrated into a peacetime economy thanks to fish cages and seaweed nets." Blah, blah, blah.

And you know what I say to that?

I say, the only economic equality we care about is the kind that gets us liquid on four or five million dollars of stock, with proceeds turned into cash.

Don't get all hot around the necktie, Hassie.

You know I can't resist my little quips.

It's my trader mentality.

I do the same thing with the sheik.

I'm always givin' him little cracks like, "You've gotta start taking notes and make believe you're doing something. You gotta have a log...called this person, made this meeting, advised on this."

So in other words, let's say AVEN goes to fifteen dollars, and the option package ya end up exercising makes two million.

Even if you're the trade minister of a place where anything goes, you still have to make it look like you actually did something. You have to create a sense of transaction...which we can do between your bank, and my company here in Vanuatu, where Jimmy is gonna park some stock.

I can say this, 'cause we're all friends, and we all prefer to conduct business overseas in places where, for lack of a better word, there's a minimum of oversight.

But before we get started, Jimmy's gotta tell Sheik Ali about the 89th Air Wing, and the VIPs he used to fly for the Air Force out of D.C.

I was tellin' Ali about how the 89th flies diplomats and foreign leaders around.

So I was sayin' to Ali, "Next time you're in Washington, when you hop a ride on one of our VC-9s, you can say, 'I have a business partner who used to fly one of these,'" so he can't say I dragged him over here to introduce him to some average nitwit. I introduce him to one that marries scientists that fly in Air Force jets with international aid delegations to meet with officials in Washington.

Can you believe this guy?

Most of us want blondes with big tits — but not our friend Jimmy.

He likes 'em packed with poison, having to pass through sixteen security checkpoints before they can get to their office.

And it's perfect, 'cause while she oversees the cannery, the cold storage warehouse and the fish cages and such, we'll oversee the profits.

Hey, if she can convert seaweed into gel that they put in food and medicine, we can find a way to turn our friend Hassie into a home run.

And it couldn't be better, 'cause she's expert at using all those international welfare programs, like USAID's Matching Grants Program, which will cut our initial capital investment in half.

So when he gives you all of that mumbo jumbo about establishing a safe and environmentally sustainable food source for the Philippines, remember, our poster boy is just another pea in the pod.

Wait. Wait.

Jimmy, what did you say?

Sheik Ali and you have similar environmental concerns regarding the threat of cyanide fishing to traditional fishing grounds?

Really?

Look at that.

I just learned something new.

No, seriously —

I didn't know a little underwater squirt could bring a whole school down.

When ya put it like that, it makes sense.

Like, why catch 'em one by one when you can bag a shit load, with a detonation or some poison?

It's fast. It's easy.

Like an underwater I.E.D.

You know what, this is actually good, 'cause it gives you another thing in common.

Since your people in Indonesia and Mindanao would rather use cyanide and dynamite than fish hooks, we could say your project does more than unite Muslim interests and save the coastline...it gives insurgents in Southeast Asia a means by which they can collude in an open environment, without having to do it underground.

I think we'll leave that out of our press release, though.

Can you just see the headlines?

"Muslims With Cyanide Poison Water."

Or, "Muslims With Dynamite Conduct Mass Executions."

One thing is for sure, it would make all the news wires.

I don't think it will help with liquidity, though.

So that's not going to be disclosed.

What we're going to do instead, 'cause it's better if there's perceived volume, is we're gonna announce a hundred million in projected sales for the first year — or whatever fluff — which means a seven dollar return per share.

That's my idea of nettin' haul, and puttin' some real business down.

And while we're on the subject of drivin' the revenue line, I'm assuming that the one thing we can conclude tonight is that we're gonna let Malik's brokers start pitching Aqua Venture tomorrow.

Like I said to Malik before you arrived, "I don't think Hassie is inclined to tell them to go fuck themselves if they've got firepower and are ready to go. Though he may want a little more of a comfort level with people he doesn't know."

Which is why I talked them into taking a partial — a partial payment, which is guaranteed by Malik and me, since we're all friends.

If it doesn't work, we'll make them give you your stock back, and they won't have a beef with that.

As I so fondly like to say, "The real wealth in the world is made from writing the sell tickets."

So let's give the sheik a short and sweet one, so we can get down to the business of how we're gonna get our retail program underway —

[END OF SIDE B]

Tape 4F 6/19/06
SideA

[RESUME]

Yeah, yeah.
He likes to play the straight arrow.
Did you hear his presentation to the sheik? "Gee," "Wow,"

"Golly," "Gosh," "No way!" That's his game, but I saw the little spark there in the back of his brain. See, I know how the animal thinks. You know what they say, "Birds of a feather..."

What was the comment that sparked him?

Remember when I said, "Hassie if we get the volume pumping, you have to throw your weight around at the company. Maybe you can get an S3 or an SB2 registration statement on your shares." Ergo, that's what stewing in his brain right now. When Hassie said his payday was nine months down the pike, his wheels were already turning on getting his mosque mates on the board to file a registration statement.

So now he's thinking about how many more shares he can free up for potential liquidity, to go along with the project.

What Hassie was thinking was, "Okay, I may only have two or three hundred thousand shares of free trading, but I've got two or three million of the other which won't come alive for nine months or ten months."

So what I put in the back of Hassie's mind is — and he understands exactly what I understand — that if there's four million shares of net buying activity coming in, he doesn't have enough shares to fill that buying. See?

So now Hassie is sitting back there in the guesthouse stewing over the concept of all this liquidity and fucking forcing the company to file a registration statement, unlocking his shares. That's what Hassie's looking at right now, 'cause that's what I'd be looking at.

That's why he said he needed to "digest" our proposals.

He ain't digesting! He's fucking with the liquidity in his own brain!

You follow where I'm headed?

That's what he's stewing about right now.

You wouldn't have known that, but I picked it up.

I could hear the adding machine in his brain goin' ka-ching!

[REDACTED]

No, no. You're right.

I don't know if I would go so far as to say it drags on in vain, but these are the problems you run into when you're dealing with inexperience.

You know I always say, "The best way to close a deal is to make your customer think it was his idea to finish it."

That's why I told Hassie, "Go back and digest, and we'll talk in a couple of hours," and if he's still not ready to commit, I'll have my Aussie piss in his ear. You know, this is the same category as Rupert Murdoch and Kerry Packer.

So if I says, "Rod, go blow a little smoke up his ass, 'cause y'know I'm trying to get something from him," he'll have him on a string.

And Hassie knows precisely who he's dealing with, 'cause Rod makes news five times a week there.

You're dealing with billions on a personal level. Okay?

So what I'm trying to say is, the deck can sort of be stacked, even if we have to show a little sizzle to get what we want, 'cause Rod is well trained to do us a favor.

He'll butter Hassie's ass a little. Rod can tell him, "I know a couple of guys that can get things kicked off. They're guys sitting with a bunch of lunatic traders worth hundreds, tens of millions of dollars. They'll do you a favor.

It's not a gamble so they don't give a fuck.

And if ya need someone to jump in and buy a hundred thousand shares so it don't look stupid like you're doing all the volume, and you want it kicked off like you're not kicking it off, I'll help you out — I don't give a shit. But ya gotta do the retail deal with my buddy if you want me to get behind you on this."

You're right, I agree.

We can't work with restricted stock, 'cause we can't trade it.

This is the reason we don't sit here and own a broker dealer, 'cause I don't wanna be fettered by any particular regulations which preclude me from certain activities...which nothing does.

But take it from me, at minimum you'll get some of his free trading shares to pay for the Internet promotion.

Who cares if you can't do it?

Just sell 'em out for whatever you can get.

When nothing happens, I'll tell him you can send out a million e-mails and nobody gives a fuck anymore, since the stock promotion business is focused back to retail anyways.

He won't know the difference.

So I'll get him on the Internet deal.

That's at a minimum.

At a maximum, he'll get some of his group to come up to the plate and deliver some additional shares for the brokerage side before he talks with Rod telephonically tomorrow.

If not, I'll get Rod to tell him this, and power that, and we'll get him on that too, one way or the other. And you know Rod, even though I would never let him invest in this deal, he knows how put his money where his mouth is.

He ain't bashful.

Hold on a minute while I grab the phone.

Hello?

Hey, this is early for you.

The Eastern District of New York called?

And they think what?

That I'm the secret owner of Solomon Blarney and Myers Shellac?

Well, tell them to have fun proving that.

I don't own anything.

I don't even own the shoes on my feet.

Wait...what?

Ritchie Gallo hired you to defend him?

And he's talking?

Oh, this is no good —

PILE, COTTON & PIKE

Counselors at Law

One Battery Park Plaza

New York, NY 10004-1486

James T. Koben

(212) 904-4677

June 20, 2006

LEGAL AND CONFIDENTIAL

Patrick Fitzpatrick, Esq.

Assistant United States Attorney

One St. Andrews Plaza

New York, New York 10007

Re: Conner Skilling

<u>Our File No: 867.2</u>

Dear Pat:

Conner Skilling was involved with the following companies which may or may not have resulted in criminal activity. However, he may be accused by others of being involved in market manipulation or other stock fraud activity. We are therefore requesting that these companies be included as part of the existing cooperation agreement, dated April 15, 1995, between your office and our client.

Myers, Shellac & Davidson Investment Group

Solomon Blarney Investment Partners

Equitable Catheter and Cistern (ECCS)

Electric CAT-Scan Technologies (ECAT)

Vantage Properties (VPRP)

American Technologies Exploration (ATEX)

Alcohol Censors (ALCR)

Bio-Kronology (BKTK)

Global International (GLIN)

Worldview Entertainment (WVET)

As you know, Mr. Skilling's letter agreement with your office specifically states that he will not be prosecuted further for any of the crimes originally listed in his cooperation agreement, including financial crimes related to the following publicly traded securities: BPRT (Beachside Entertainment), PALT (Palliative Management Systems), ASWE (Associated Software), INMED (Innovation Medical) and Big Boy Brands (BBIU).

Because Mr. Skilling's truthful disclosure of ongoing criminal activity currently includes highly sensitive information on activities of individuals who might use violence, force, and intimidation against the interests of the United States, we believe a quick and equitable resolution to this problem in the form of an addendum to cover the additional securities mentioned would be in the best interest of all parties, so that Mr. Skilling can confidently proceed with current undercover investigations.

Very truly yours,

James Koben

U.S. Department of Justice
Southern District of New York

June 20, 2006

James T. Koben
Pile, Cotton and Pike
One Battery Park Plaza
New York, New York 10004

Re: Conner Skilling

Dear Jim:

I am writing to acknowledge that I received your letter dated June 21, 2006, listing several additional companies with which Mr. Skilling was involved. Based on our conversations today, it is my understanding that Mr. Skilling has stated that he did not engage in any criminal activity with respect to these companies, but believes other persons may accuse him of such criminal activities. These companies therefore do not need to be listed in Mr. Skilling's cooperation agreement. However, we have taken note of the companies listed in your letter, and will contact the Eastern District to advise them of Mr. Skilling's relationship with this office.

Please call me if you have any questions.

Very truly yours,

PATRICK H. FITZPATRICK
Assistant United States Attorney

From: CW1
Sent: Tuesday, June 20, 2006, 11:23:56 am
To: Agent Farrow
Cc: Agent Lossman, AUSA Patrick Fitzpatrick, AUSA Jason Varlet
Subject: EXPLOSIVE NEW INFORMATION

Greetings from Port Vila:

Last night Jamal Hassim revealed that Muslims in the Philippines commonly use cyanide for fishing purposes. The easy availability of this deadly,
water-soluble poison amongst terrorists and terrorist sympathizers could
signal a massive attack on U.S. food and water supplies. It was also
revealed that Philippine fishermen regularly use commercial and military-
grade dynamite to kill massive numbers of fish, another strong indicator
that combatants from Mindanao have the mastery, weapons, and capability
to stage a devastating act of terrorism in the U.S. Jamal indicates that
rogue members of the Philippine military may have sold large stockpiles
of Goma 2 Eco dynamite and other types of explosives to these fishermen, many of whom are "former" enemy combatants.

Special Alert:

It was revealed in a private, breakaway conversation, that Jamal Hassim's
infiltration of the 89th Air Wing is still ongoing, through friendships he
continues to maintain with Air Force officers who work in that squadron.

The promotion plans for Aqua Venture and Bangsamoro Seaweed should
be complete by the end of business today. Negotiations have gone a bit
slower than expected, because Hassim needs to free up more of his
restricted stock into free trading shares, so that he can pay for the
crooked boiler room and Internet promotions that he requested. He
assures me that the he's "most eager to do business" regarding both promotional avenues, and will do so just as soon as he can get the board

members from Aqua Venture to file for S3 and SB2 conversions, and loan him some of their own free trading shares for the promotion payment, until his restricted shares are freed up. He told me that he anticipates being able to confirm full payment today or tomorrow, at which time we will go forward with a stock transfer into one of my shell companies.

Ahn Hassim arrived back on the property with my wife this morning. Candy tried to delay her for a few more hours so I could finish up my business with Jamal, but she became very "agitated" and insisted she "must go home." She is currently in the guesthouse. As you are aware, I consider her dangerous and highly alert to possible discovery. For this reason, I will endeavor to conclude this investigation quickly, so that I can make myself available as soon as possible for the grand jury.

Jim Koben tells me that Pat's office is concerned that my cover may be blown because of an investigation by the U.S. Attorney's office from the Eastern District, which could potentially expose my family to extraordinary risk. If you have any further trouble regarding these false allegations that have surfaced against me, let me know. I HAVE A VERY NOVEL THOUGHT FOR YOU ON THIS MATTER IF YOU NEED ANY ASSISTANCE.

Regards to the family — and try to get some sleep.

Tape 5A 6/20/06
Side A

[REDACTED]

What are you doing here?

What do you mean that's what you wanna ask me?

For God sakes, I told you already, I got enough jet fuel with the husband from a strategic point of view. I don't have no axe to grind with the wife.

No, no. Please Candy, not now. I don't want to hear no more sanctimonious bullshit about how legitimate they are. You take her high road crap too seriously. Not for nothin', but you've been sold down the river.

I don't care what you believe.

You don't know nothin' about business. See, I know the whole story, which you don't, and I can tell you — no one is that good.

I understand, you think she's a very nice woman.

And out of respect for your opinion, I've modified my plan.

Meaning, I'm gonna give her some reasonable protections here, which you can help facilitate by keeping her out of my hair. So go over to the guesthouse and have a little chitchat or a coffee klatch or whatever it is that you do. And remember, under no circumstances are you to let her come over here while I confer with her husband, 'cause this guy's a little edgy of a guy, who's somewhat quirky, from what I can construe.

What I'm saying is there's a little bit of resistance, so I need to explore this situation delicately on a personal level without any interference.

Kapishe?

Come on, Candy. Give me a fuckin' break.

This should be like second nature.

I never heard you cry over what was gonna happen to the Phillips or the Stephens or any other ones we worked on. You don't even remember most of their names.

Oh, and don't give me that crap you never got to know any of them on such a personal level.

How about the Caputo's? Joan was in your wedding party.

John was my best man.

Alls I'm saying is I don't understand why you keep harpin' on this issue when I gave you my word the Hassim woman is not the focus of this case.

Let me tell you what, if you're gonna eavesdrop and try and pick up bits and pieces of my conversations with Fitzie, you should be more thorough about it, then.

I never said she was a high-value target.

And frankly speaking, as long as I can cut a satisfactory deal with Hassie today, which will likely be the case, all this legwork won't be nothin' but air.

Now wait a minute.

I don't want to hear no more speeches about your conscience.

I'm going to explain something to you. Okay?

We're in a situation where we're over the coals, so to speak, which means we gotta bring something to the table so we can continue to have some control before the bottom drops out. I didn't want to tell you this, but let's just say there's been a recent hiccup with couple of stateside situations where you're president of the board.

Oh, you want a "for instance?"

Does Worldview Entertainment sound familiar?

Yeah well, it's sounding familiar to some other people too, who you don't want to be having your name. So don't give me none of this drama about what you can or can't do. 'Cause I'm gonna tell you, we're doin' this to protect our ass. And remember, it's our ass that comes first. Do you understand?

Okay then.

Let's get ourselves together.

Now, what you need to do is straighten yourself out and go over and sit with your friend for a nice tête-à-tête.

And make sure to do it with your game face smiling.

This is for your benefit.

[RESUME]

There he is, Mr. Hassim!

Always a pleasure!

Especially today, 'cause this is when we pick our prime tomatoes.

What I mean is, things never grow overnight, they need to grow like any relationship.

It's like I said to Malik last night, I don't know if you heard me, but I says, "You got to schmooze. It may take a couple of days, or maybe even a week, but the more seeds we plant, the more vegetables will sprout. And when you plant these bigger things, like we're working on with Jamal, you have to look at it like we're planting a harvest."

But now we're ripe.

I brought you to the trough, and now it's time to drink.

You have to admit, I could sell ice to an Eskimo.

Exhibit number one — my Australian last night after I put him under direct cross-examination. You heard it yourself — under direct district attorney style cross-examination, he says, "I'm ready to write a check from my discretionary account. Announce the deal on international wires. 'Australian Insurance Giant HIG invests in Philippine fish farms. CEO Rodney Flitch announces a twenty million dollar investment in Bangasmoro Seaweed and Aqua Venture LLC.' "

That's what he said.

Now even though he didn't go near it, being very discreet and all, he assumes that because I was instrumental in getting his tranche placed forthwith for par, you're on board with my business plan and compensation package.

No, no.

There's no more time to ruminate my friend.

The story has been told, the table has been set.

You have to get comfortable with that.

There's no more time to say, "Should I pass or play the game?" 'Cause I already told him, "We got the money deal worked out."

By the way, did you notice the segue I used with Rod?

"The reason it took Hassim five days to make up his mind to do this deal is because he admonished me to be accurate in telling you what we can do. So, you know, that's the reason it took a while."

So we transitioned out of the dilly-dally like you're not responsible...like you made his interests important enough that you took extra time to make the commitment.

Okay?

[TAPE BREAK]

Yeah, I understand.

You don't want any trouble.

I know what you mean. I mean, I don't want pictures taken and all that nonsense, 'cause that's bad stuff. I don't blame you.

You'd rather sit on it forever than have that.

That, that's a ticket to get pinched for twenty years with that, and people dangling out windows and that shit.

Yeah, well we don't want any part of that either, because we escaped that ten years ago.

We escaped and moved on to other things.

Let me ask you a question.

Suppose we were able to construct a situation whereby you were able to support your endeavor without a promotion, where investment was, for lack of a better word — indirect?

'Cause we have a few situations here, okay, insofar as your contacts are concerned, which intrigued me with what you were doing, which is why I brought you here in the first place. And these are long-time friends, with de facto control of property, which, on a global market, can be sold for a hundred and fifty times what we spend.

So what I'm looking for, what I'm basically looking for, since we're friends, and this is sort of oddball — sort of a one off situation — is access to specialized markets that you have relationships with. It's very unusual, which you'll understand when I show you the — thing.

So let's just say, using a hypothetical, let's just say, I had some systems that could be of interest to investors on your island, you know, with the kind of guys it would be awkward for me to deal with direct.

Remember I said when we first started to chat, even if you do nothing, I still want to use you as an intermediary for...for other reasons. Do you recall me saying that?

Well this is what I meant.

This is what you call profit and firepower all rolled into one, and it don't set off compliance whistles on the floor of the stock exchange.

You don't have to worry about market surveillance reporting sudden block bids from fucking Bermudian hedge funds, or fruit-cakes manufacturing a piece of news now and then.

And there's no hard sell.

There's a built-in customer base already stewing in their own juices, with a high level of interest, ready to invest.

Of course I know what these are used for.

No different than dynamite, cyanide, and botulism — and much more profitable, I might add.

This one alone brings a quarter million on the black market, and we got a thousand more just like it.

Give me your poor, your ignorant, your diseased, your under-fed, no standing army, no electricity, no reliable water supply — put one of these babies on their shoulder, and bam! Instant credibility.

The problem is I need a distribution base.

And this time there won't be no dog and ponies involved.

Your guys in Mindanao will be salivating for these the way my German Shepherd salivates for a rib roast. And from there we'll get referrals to their contacts in Egypt, Malaysia, Morocco, Chechnya — Afghanistan.

The reaction will be off the meter.

And your pitch will be quicker than a cup of coffee.

There'll be no need for the curveballs, the fastballs and the changeup, 'cause it's a foregone conclusion.

And once you hook us in with the right operators, there's effectively no maximum, 'cause I have the supply and the coded account, so it's just unlimited. More money than you'll ever see in your life, no matter how much fish stock and seaweed you sell.

You would never do it, no matter how much is in it for you?

There's more than money involved here, my friend.

I'm a genius, and you know why?

'Cause you won't be able to say "no," after you peruse my offering, since I'm always prepared with instruments that are dressed nicely with a de minimus risk to me.

As they say in New York, and as I'm so fond of saying, "The more dogs hooked up to the sled, the better the sled runs."

So when I saw you in Sydney, I classified you as a big Alaskan malamute.

And it's worked out wonderfully, 'cause no matter what kind of race you throw in, ipso facto, I win.

You want to know how I can do that when you categorically refuse?

I suggest you withhold your resistance until after you take a peek at your option package.

Let's start by looking behind door number one, and you'll begin to see the craft and the handiwork.

Let's say we start with the comment you just made about going to the FBI.

That's checkmate, partner.

See, I am the FBI.

Mandated to record state of mind, with tapes like this — which makes me a treacherous little prick in more ways than one — and you guilty of mail fraud, wire fraud, stock fraud, insider trading, treason, terrorism, and whatever else my crew can dream up if I confirm that this case is a "go."

And, just for your information, they like to dream big.

They'll have you working with bin Laden, planning to poison Mrs. Magilacutty and blowing up Wall Street while running a stock fraud scheme to pay for the whole shebang in less than a week.

You don't believe that?

Let me tell you something, partner, my colleagues in New York are drafting your indictment right now, based on some mutual due diligence we've been working on together.

Let's face it, you and your wife do make a good retail story.

That's right. Your wife.

And it couldn't be better, what with her credentials as a chemist, and her history aiding Muslim fighters. The floodgates will start opening the minute we issue the press release.

It'll be the mother lode.

Oh, it don't matter that I don't have her on tape, my friend.

I have you listening to all my little quips.

And it's perfect, 'cause alls I need to maximize credibility is some wormy language and a tape recorder.

You'll need a defense team, at least ten years of your life and every penny you ever made to defend yourself. And while you do, your wife will get interrogated by a bunch of Kackistanis who'll put their cigarettes out in her ears if she don't tell them what they want to hear; and there won't be nothin' you or any of your liberal, do-good-er, help the-world, defend-the-downtrodden organizations will be able to do about it, 'cause she'll be an enemy combatant — since she's not one of us.

Which means you'll never know where she is.

Her location will be a matter of national security.

So you'll write to Human Rights Watch, the American Red Cross and the ACLU from your isolation cell, and no one will give a damn, 'cause they'll have all seen your press...

"Fish Fiends Plan Bio-Terror Attacks"

"WMD at the CDC."

They won't be predisposed to move along with your particular endeavor when they've got so many other more compelling cases on their plate, like all the Aqua Venture investors from your mosque with their assets frozen by the Treasury Department being detained as material witnesses, for three years, or five years, or until the war on terrorism is over, crying about their civil rights.

That's whose cases will get priority.

Maybe even a sympathetic article in *The New York Times.*

Not that it will matter, especially if one of them cracks — which people tend to do after they've been basted and broiled in a federal detention center for a while.

Personally, I'm optimal for a three-week maturity on Malik.

He'll be singing louder than Maria Callas, telling them anything they want to hear about the "private conversations" he had with you off-tape, so he can cut a deal.

What does he give a fuck?

He don't know you, and six months home detention is better

than twenty years in the penitentiary.

At your trial he'll be the best friend you never had.

And if you think for one minute all your years in the Air Force is gonna give you credibility; you'll be right, but not in the way you'd expect.

My boys in New York will say that your perfect record makes you the most nefarious type of high-level Qaeda recruit, where nobody knows from nothing, nice and quiet, slipped under the radar, infiltrated into high-level security positions in the West, waiting for activation.

I'll be called a patriot for risking my life to uncover the biggest and most advanced sleeper cell since 9/11.

You'll be the next Mohammad Atta, on my word moving forward.

And it's the perfect switch-up, 'cause they won't look at what I'm doing, even if they figure it out.

They can't. They won't.

We got too many bodies buried together, and the last thing they want is an explosion.

Justice doesn't work that way?

You are naïve my friend.

Justice is a business.

The best one in the world, and you know why?

'Cause there ain't no risks. You don't need to worry about organizing a profit and loss statement or coming up with a story line that actually works. My colleagues in New York will argue, "Conspiracy is always inchoate, like, it's never a fully formed idea. That's why it's called conspiracy, see?"

We don't have to prove that a plan was complete, or even partially structured.

It just has to be a thought.

So your lawyers will argue, "But the criminal thoughts all came from your witness!"

And you know what my colleagues will say?

They'll say, "It's the government's job to stop crime before it happens. It's our right to expose people with guilty ideas — especially today."

And I'll tell you what, nine times out of ten the jury will agree.

They'll be like, "We're not even looking at who said what and whether it would have happened, or if it ever could. Just walk us through it 'cause if this guy was really innocent at the first mention of anything shady, he should have run away."

And I know how you'll respond already.

You'll say, "I didn't agree to anything. No contracts were written. No agreements were signed. No money changed hands. I was just politely tolerating this man so that I could have the possibility of meeting all the rich contacts he said he had, and to see if any of them were real."

And you'll lose that argument too.

Oh, you don't think that's right?

May I suggest you take a listen to what's behind door number two.

CS: You heard it yourself, under direct district attorney style cross-examination, he says, "I'm ready to write a check, from my discretionary account. Announce the deal on international wires. 'Australian Insurance Giant HIG invests in Philippine fish farms. CEO Rodney Flitch announces a twenty million dollar investment in Bangsamoro Seaweed and Aqua Venture LLC.' " That's what he said. Now even though he didn't go near it, being very discreet and all, he assumes that because I was instrumental in getting his tranche placed forthwith for par, you're on board with my business plan and compensation package.

JH: I need to think about it, I...

CS: No, no. There's no more time to ruminate my friend. The story has been told, the table has been set. You have to get comfortable with that. There's no more time to say, "Should I pass or play the game?" 'Cause I already told him, "I got the money deal worked out." By the way, did you notice the segue I used with Rod? "The reason it took Hassim five days to make up his mind to do this deal is because he admonished me to be accurate in telling you what we can do. So, you know, that's the reason it took a while." So we transitioned out of the dilly-dally, like you're not responsible...like you made his interests important enough that you took extra time to make the commitment. Okay?

JH: Okay.

Gotcha!

There you are, right here, today, agreeing to all of my proposals.

It don't matter that it took me five days to get you to say "okay," or that "okay" might not mean "I agree," that it might mean, "I heard what you said."

That's a matter of interpretation, or "inference" as they call it.

The government will say, "okay" means, "I do."

I do a life sentence in a Super-Max.

You can infer from that and convict. You're permitted to do that in a conspiracy case. And the jury will likely agree, especially after they hear about all your holy-roller enterprises and extracurricular Muslim activities.

Take my word for it, they'll throw the book at you and walk out of the courtroom feeling like they served your three tours in Iraq.

And don't even think about pleading entrapment.

We're too sophisticated and masterful to allow you to have any real chance to fight back.

See, the key is never to construct something where there's not deniability...plausible deniability, like, "We didn't entrap this guy."

Here's the proof, behind door number three.

Conspiracy to manipulate the stock price of two separate companies...Aqua Venture and Bangsamoro Seaweed.

You got to have that.

Otherwise it could be awkward, like, you could argue, "I was an innocent who was inadvertently hoodwinked into a trap."

So the two indictments give us a nice little layer of insulation, since each one demonstrates criminal intent — which cancels out your ability to use an entrapment defense.

Not that you would have had a Chinaman's chance at winning against us anyways, since we only lose two percent of the time.

And those are real numbers.

That's why I'm such a clever little fella.

I got a gig with the best rig in town, with discretion to do anything I want.

Oh really?

You don't believe the United States government would rely on the word of a man like me?

I have two words for that:

Ahmed Chalabi.

Which is not to say he's got any more talent, 'cause from a situational perspective, he got the benefit of having a little bit of ride.

But have no doubt about it.

There's plethora of people in jail right now that could tell you I'm very active in coming up with prospective proposals for the FBI.

And it goes splendidly.

The public feels protected. The Justice Department gets to pretend it's actually doing something. And I get to continue to operate, nice and quiet, with colleagues who are favorably inclined.

So the groundwork is set wonderfully.

And it's a nice quid pro quo. 'Cause whenever people say, "Why didn't you save us from WorldCom and Enron and Global Crossing and Adelphia, my boys can say, "Look, we saved you from Stockgate. Over a hundred brokers and promoters in jail for the largest stock fraud conspiracy in the history of the United States."

And now when people complain, "Why can't you protect us from bin Laden and al-Zawhahiri?" my boys can say, "Look! We've saved you from a conspiracy that would have caused the worst terrorist disaster the world has ever seen.

We saved you from Jamal and Ahn Hassim!"

So go ahead, try telling my boys I'm selling Manpads out of my spare bedroom.

They won't want to hear the blither and the blather any more than they wanted hear about Rodney Flitch during the Stockgate trials.

All they'll want to hear is how many times you said yes, yup, uh huh, and right. Okay?

'Cause they understand what I understand.

At the end of the day it's the sizzle that sells the steak.

So, what I'm saying is, I don't care how you do it

If you want to do it the right way, we can get fees in a very crafty manner in a tax-exempt environment, dispensed to anyone we wanna dispense to.

And if you want to do it the wrong way, I've got a really good grasp and understanding.

This is a masterpiece I've constructed.

'Cause I'm gonna make wool off this lamb no matter what.

It's just which manner that I do it...

FEDERAL BUREAU OF INVESTIGATION
Date of transcription 06/21/06

Source, who is in a position to testify, provided the following information:

1. One (1) audiocassette containing a consensually recorded conversation with JAMAL HASSIM on 6/16/06; and

2. One (1) audiocassette containing two consensually recorded conversations between source and JAMAL HASSIM on 6/17/06 and one between source and JAMAL HASSIM and MELVIN SMALLS on 6/17/06; and

3. One (1) audiocassette containing four consensually recorded conversations, two between source and MELVIN SMALLS on 6/18/06, two between source and JAMAL HASSIM on 6/18/06, and one between source and JAMAL HASSIM and MELVIN SMALLS on 6/19/06; and

4. One (1) audiocassette containing a consensually recorded conversation with JAMAL HASSIM on 6/20/06; and

5. A fax cover page from JAMAL HASSIM dated 6/16/06 and attached Draft Business Plan for AQUA VENTURE, INC.; and

6. Cover page from BANGSAMORO SEAWEED INC. to CONNER SKILLING and attached Financial Statements for BANGSAMORO SEAWEED INC. from 12/31/2004 and 2005; and

7. A copy of an article published in the MINDANEO SUN-STAR related to BANGSAMORO SEAWEED dated 4/28/2002; and

8. Copies of business cards of JAMAL HASSIM of AQUA VENTURE and AHN HASSIM of AQUA VENTURE and BANGSAMORO SEAWEED

For Immediate Release
Date: June 22, 2006
Contact: Jason Varlet (212) 384-2715

1. FBI – NEW YORK OFFICE – PRESS RELEASE

The United States Attorney for the Southern District of New York, the Assistant Director in Charge of the New York Office of the Federal Bureau Of Investigation ("FBI") and the Homeland Security Secretary, joined by the Director of Enforcement of the United States Securities and Exchange Commission ("SEC"), and the President of the National Association of Securities Dealers ("NASD"), announced that 130 defendants, including members of

Al Qaeda, have been charged with securities fraud and related crimes, which include conspiracy to commit acts of terrorism on civilians, counseling others to wage war against the United States, and use of firearms, explosives, and weapons of mass destruction in furtherance of violent crimes.

Three indictments and four criminal complaints unsealed today in Manhattan federal court allege fraud in connection with the publicly traded securities of two companies, Aqua Venture and Bangsamoro Seaweed. Included among the defendants are three alleged members of Al Qaeda: including a former New York City Police detective, an Air Force Reservist serving in the 314th South Carolina Air Wing, and a Muslim cleric. Officers, directors and other "insiders" of the companies issuing securities involved in the frauds were also arrested for providing material support to a terrorist organization. The various schemes devised by this network anticipated raising approximately $50 million in investment capital, to be diverted to Philippine jihadists, who planned to use the money to purchase explosives and biological weapons in furtherance of a planned terror attack against the United States. Many tens of millions more would have been raised had the schemes been completed. According to U.S. District Attorney MARGARITA NEY, this is the largest number of defendants ever arrested at one time on securities fraud and terrorism charges, and the largest number ever arrested in a criminal case of any kind. In coordination with today's arrests, search warrants were executed at one location in New York and four locations in Atlanta, including the Oulel-Albab Mosque, where it is alleged the scheme was conceived.

Twenty-one of the defendants in this scheme are also charged with participating in a RICO Enterprise consisting of members and associates of Abu Sayaf and The Moro Islamic Liberation Front. It is alleged they planned to perpetrate massive securities fraud through corrupt small cap companies by forging corrupt alliances with members and associates of the Taliban and Al Qaeda; controlling and infiltrating broker dealers; conspiring with issuers of securities and individual stock brokers; and scheming to defraud union pension plans by using traditional boiler room operations and current Internet techniques. The planned profits of these crimes were to be used to support acts of violence, including murder, through the use of explosives and the dissemination of deadly biological agents in the nation's water parks.

The racketeering defendants include, among others: MELVIN SMALLS, a/k/a "Malik el-Tiberius," a retired New York City detective, and associate of Al Qaeda, who is alleged to have attempted to corruptly exploit former colleagues at the Detective's Endowment Association and other New York area unions by offering bribes and kickbacks in order to secure investment for Bangsamoro Seaweed and Aqua Venture LLC; enlist the services of crews of brokers at various brokerage houses to manipulate these stocks; and use corrupt Internet promotions in furtherance of the stock manipulation scheme. SHEIK TARAK YOUSSOF, a/k/a "Imam Tarak," a cleric with the Oulel-Albab Mosque, and associate of Al Qaeda, is also charged with RICO violations. In his capacity as an officer of Aqua Venture, he is alleged to have incited members of his congregation to wage war against the United States by investing in the corrupt securities, Aqua Venture and Bangsamoro Seaweed, knowing the stock was being manipulated by "insiders," who planned to use the profits to support international jihad. The RICO Enterprise is alleged to have been engineered by JAMAL M. HASSIM, a/k/a "Jimmy Hassim," an Air Force major and officer of Aqua Venture and Bangsamoro Seaweed, who, as a secret associate of Abu Sayaf, the Moro Liberation Front, and Al Qaeda, infiltrated some of the highest security zones of the United States Air Force, including the SAM FOX air wing, which transports congressional leaders, foreign leaders, and diplomats.

In addition to racketeering charges regarding the corrupt manipulation and promotion of Aqua Venture and Bangsamoro Seaweed, which were fraudulently rigged for the benefit of insiders and corrupt brokers, Major Hassim is also charged with treason and spying for a foreign power; which he is alleged to have carried out by collecting photos of various national and international Air Force bases. These bases include Pago Pago, Alice Springs, Australia, Grand Forks, North Dakota and Minot, North Dakota. Exterior aerial photos of various U.S. fighter planes, photos of U.S. transport planes, and interior photos of the Military Air Mission hangar at Andrews Air Force base, including pictures of VC-20A, VC-20H, VC-37A, C-40B, C-3A, and VC-9 jets utilized by the Special Air Mission (SAM FOX) Air Wing were also collected by Major Hassim in furtherance of the alleged scheme. Major Hassim is also charged with conspiracy to use firearms and conspiracy to use explosives and biological agents in furtherance of violent crimes against civilians in the United States; conspiracy to hijack a U.S. Air Force jet; conspiracy to commit murder, and training others to commit acts of violence through the use of laser tag guns. It is alleged that Mr. Hassim and other conspirators in the scheme used the names of fish, mollusk, and seaweed types, such as carp, blood cockle, grouper, bangus, and Zanzibar weed, to signal plans for securities fraud and mass homicide in furtherance of global jihad.

In addition to the defendants named in today's indictment, DR.

AHN H. HASSIM, a Philippine foreign national and research fellow with the Centers for Disease Control specializing in chemical and biological agents, including botulism and cyanide, has also been arrested in connection with this case. The Pentagon announced that she is being held in an undisclosed location, and that no formal charges will be filed until her interrogation is complete.

Today's charges are the result of a highly successful, weeklong emergency undercover operation conducted by the FBI's New York office. The undercover investigation involved, among other things, surveillance, the use of undercover purchases of securities, the use of court-authorized eavesdropping devices and the use of a cooperating witness, who posed as a willing participant in ongoing criminal schemes.

The White House praised the efforts of all the law enforcement agencies involved, and particularly commended the outstanding investigative efforts of the FBI. Assistant United States Attorneys PATRICK J. FITZPATRICK and JASON C. VARLET are in charge of the prosecutions.

The charges contained in the indictments and complaints are merely accusations, and the defendants are presumed innocent unless and until proven guilty.

3:36 p.m. ET
June 22
TOP STORY FROM AP
US Arrests Air Force Officer for Operating Terror Ring

PORT VILA, Vanuatu (AP) — A ranking Air Force major was arrested early this morning for his role in the operation of a global jihadist organization with links to Islamic extremists in the Philippines, Indonesia, and the United States. His wife, a well-known Filipino scientist, was also arrested in connection with the case. The two were said to be planning a series of attacks on military and civilian targets in the U.S. Officials from the Justice Department announced that a dictionary computer operated by the National Security Agency (NSA) provided the first major break in the case while conducting routine automated surveillance of international phone calls.

Officers and Directors of Two NASDAQ Companies Indicted for Terrorism, Fraud
By REUTERS
Published: June 22, 2006
Filed at 3:54 p.m. ET

NEW YORK (Reuters)

Investor confidence in two NASDAQ small cap stocks plummeted after prosecutors in New York announced the arrest of all senior staff members and many key investors associated with Bangsamoro Seaweed and Aqua Venture on charges of stock fraud and conspiracy to commit acts of terrorism. FBI agents arrested board members from both companies at their homes in pre-dawn raids timed to coincide with the arrests of the board president, Major Jamal M. Hassim and his wife, Dr. Ahn H. Hassim, CEO of both companies, on an island in the South Pacific, where the two were attempting to arrange additional funding for what prosecutors have characterized as "fraudulent companies" created for the sole purpose of supplying Islamic militants with technical and financial support. According to prosecutors, that support was about to culminate in a series of devastating bio-terror attacks aimed at a variety of public and private institutions, including water parks and various high-consumption products produced by the U.S. food processing industry, including soft drinks, fruit juices, milk, and processed tomato products. At a press conference today U.S. District Attorney Margarita Ney noted that investigators had been watching this plot for only a week before moving in to make the arrests. "We stopped this conspiracy just days before it was about to result in mass murder on an unimaginable scale," she said. The White House released a statement that the President had been briefed on the details of the plot "for days," and that its deadly intentions had been averted "just in time."

Friday, June 23, 2006

DOZENS NAMED IN STOCK FRAUD LINKED TO AL QAEDA

Prosecutors have charged dozens of people, many associated with the Oulel-Albab Mosque, located in Atlanta, Georgia, with using stock manipulation and fraud to finance bio-terror attacks on water parks across the country, in a scheme that federal authorities are calling Al Qaeda's most aggressive foray into fundraising and coordinated acts of domestic terrorism since 9/11.

The authorities said their investigation swept up several high-ranking "homegrown" members of the Qaeda network, including an

Air Force reservist, Major Jamal M. Hassim and his wife, Dr. Ahn H. Hassim, a foreign fellow at the Centers for Disease Control in Atlanta, who is alleged to have provided technical and financial support to Abu Sayaf and other terrorist groups operating in the South Pacific for many years. Others arrested for involvement in the Atlanta jihad network include an Indonesian born Muslim cleric, Sheik Tarak Youssof, and retired police officer Melvin Smalls, also known as Malik el-Tiberius, who served as treasurer of the New York City Detectives Union from 1992 until his retirement in 1999.

At the center of the investigation are two companies listed on the NASDAQ, Aqua Venture (AVEN) and Bangsamoro Seaweed (BMSE), which prosecutors said were created and controlled by members of Mr. Youssof's mosque as an alternative to Islamic charity organizations, which the Justice Department had effectively eliminated as a source of terror funding since the September 11th attacks. In an indictment filed in Federal District Court in Manhattan, prosecutors charged that the conspirators planned to fraudulently manipulate the stock price of Aqua Venture and Bangsamoro Seaweed through a range of schemes, from running traditional high pressure boiler room sales operations to bribing brokers and creating phony stock trades. Such tactics would artificially inflate the price of the stocks, which would then be sold at an illicit profit. According to prosecutors, the profits of this fraud were then going to be wired into secret coded overseas bank accounts for the purchase of explosives for bomb making and cyanide, a deadly water-soluble poison, which the conspirators allegedly planned to release in public pools across America, potentially causing tens of thousands of deaths.

Investigators also speculate that Dr. Ahn Hassim, a specialist in food-borne bacteria, was planning to contaminate the nation's dairy and food supplies with botulism. "Just one millionth of a gram of botulism is enough to kill an adult," observed Assistant United States Attorney Patrick J. Fitzpatrick, "Which is why the FBI and the Justice Department have taken the extraordinary step of closing down all research laboratories at the CDC until a full inventory of bacterial stockpiles is complete."

Major Hassim, whose high-level security clearance allowed him to infiltrate the elite SAM-FOX air wing, responsible for the transport of top American and international leaders, and surveil key U.S. air fields located near missile defense sites and nuclear installations, was described by Assistant United States Attorney David Varlet as "a treasonous criminal" and a "kingpin of hate against America and everything we stand for, especially our freedom."

Much of the indictment against Jamal Hassim, Tarak Youssof, and Melvin Smalls is based on taped conversations and wiretaps conducted after NSA surveillance programs identified them as individuals likely to be involved in terrorist activities. All three have been charged with treason, conspiracy to commit acts of terrorism on civilians, counseling others to wage war against the United States, and use of firearms, explosives, and weapons of mass destruction in furtherance of violent crimes. They are currently being held without bail in the high-security unit of the Manhattan Detention Center. The Homeland Security Department has raised the threat level to red due to the seriousness of the alleged plot, and continued concern that additional members from what has been described by investigators as, "The most far-reaching and sophisticated sleeper cell ever discovered in the history of the United States," may still be at large. BREAKING STORY— MUJAHEDEEN IN THE MARKET

>> Americans are trying to recover from the shock that one of our own, a decorated Air Force officer, has been implicated in the biggest domestic terror plot in the history of the United States.

>> That's right, Diane. Major Jamal Hassim, a 16-year veteran of the Air Force, was arrested yesterday in an FBI sting operation on the tiny South Pacific island of Efante, part of the island nation called Vanuatu, off the coast of Australia.

>> In a far-reaching plot, which some investigators are now calling, "Mujahedeen in the Market," a sleeper cell operating out of a mosque in Atlanta planned to artificially inflate the price of two Wall Street stocks, then use the profits to finance the biggest attack ever staged on U.S. soil, using bacteria, deadly poisons, and explosives to contaminate the nation's water and food supply and attack high value targets, including nuclear installations, located near air force bases across the country. For more on this story, we have a special report from Brian Williams.

>>Diane, the FBI and members of the Army's Special Forces conducted a pre-dawn raid on a home located on this volcanic island, which until yesterday was best known as a remote offshore tax haven. All that changed with the arrests of Air Force Major Jamal Hassim and his wife, Dr. Ahn Hassim, who were putting what my sources at the Pentagon describe as the "finishing touches" on an international terror plot with another alleged American conspirator — a former police officer from New York — who was also involved in what officials are now calling a multinational jihadist terror ring, with cells located in Vanuatu, Indonesia, the United States, and the Philippines.

>> Brian, do officials have any idea how long this terror ring was operational before it was discovered?

>> It's unclear at this time how long this network was in existence, but top officials in the State Department speculate that it could have been functioning for a number of years. They point out that one of the "fronts" used by this group to legitimize the transfer of large sums of money between the United States and Islamic guerillas in the Philippines was a business called Bangsamoro Seaweed, which has been a going concern for over a decade on the Muslim island of Mindanao. They say this group was so sophisticated that it actually convinced officials from the U.S. Agency for International Development to issue a number of matching grants to support its fraudulent businesses, which officials here in Washington now believe were nothing more than terrorist slush funds.

>> So, let me get this straight. These terrorists, who planned to attack American children in swimming parks and blow up nuclear reactors, had figured out a way to get U.S. taxpayers to fund their terror operation?

>> That appears to be the case, Diane, which is why the discovery of this cell was so shocking, and critical.

>>Do officials have any idea how close this group was to actually launching an attack?

>>I have been told that there is evidence that Major Hassim and his wife, an expert in poisons with high security clearances at the

CDC's main offices in Atlanta, had staked out a number of water parks throughout the U.S. With the summer season rapidly slipping by, it was feared that had the FBI had not acted when it did, a cyanide attack on a number of water parks across the country would have likely occurred in the next few weeks. We'll know more after an emergency, joint operation between American and Philippine military forces have captured key members of the Moro Liberation Front, an Islamic separatist group in the Philippines that the Hassims had worked with closely over the years, which was officially declared a terrorist organization yesterday by the United States. Interestingly, the Moro Liberation Front had recently entered into peace talks with the Philippine government, in a move that many here now view as a ruse, to divert attention from its true purpose.

>> I know there are a lot of parents and children out there who are breathing a sigh of relief that this plot has been averted.

>>Diane, my sources tell me that most horrifying part of this plot is that children were the obvious targets. Right now, investigators are interrogating Dr. Hassim — who is not an American citizen, and has not yet been formally charged — at an undisclosed location, in an effort to discover how close this group came to releasing botulism into the American food supply, and what food products were targeted. As you know, Former Homeland Security Director Tom Ridge has repeatedly warned that terrorists would turn to bio-terror. Unfortunately, it now appears his predictions were accurate.

>> I know we are all thankful that the FBI and the Justice Department were able to avert what might have been the biggest terror attack ever launched on U.S. soil.

>>As you know, Diane, the FBI has weathered a lot of criticism over the years for failing to prevent the September 11th attacks. Officials here say it was good old-fashioned police work that prevented this latest attack, which would have surely dwarfed the casualty count of the World Trade Center if it had been allowed to occur.

>>Brian, isn't it true that the FBI only learned about this terrorist cell because a computer in New Zealand picked up a suspicious phone call?

>> That's what is being reported, Diane. My sources tell me that the arrests of these terrorists could not have happened without the international network of powerful computer robots that collect data of interest for the NSA's highly classified global interception system, called ECHELON, which is reportedly monitoring over two million communications every hour of every day. The eavesdropping capacity of this surveillance system is so top-secret, only a few judges from the Foreign Intelligence Surveillance Court and a small number of hand-selected officials in the Justice Department have full working knowledge of its ability.

>> Computers save us from terror attacks. What will be next?

>>The deployment of new and even more powerful technology to intercept international and domestic communications passing through fiber optic cables, microwave signals, and satellites — with even less public disclosure on how these systems operate, according to my sources in the Department of Homeland Security.

Companies Attached to Terrorism Suspects Collapse

By REUTERS
Published June 23, 2006
Filed at 4:10 p.m. ET

NEW YORK (Reuters)

Share prices of both companies implicated in the biggest terror-ist fundraising scheme in U.S. history plummeted amidst persistent rumors that the U.S. would seek to investigate the personal and financial backgrounds of all investors associated with Aqua Venture and Bangsamoro Seaweed, and suspend the foreign and domestic operations of both companies until investigations of all employees, including managerial staff, is complete. "The process could take weeks," according to Patrick Fitzpatrick, lead prosecutor in the case against Jamal Hassim, Sheik Tarak Youssof, and Melvin Smalls, three of the alleged masterminds behind the "Mujahedeen in the Market" scheme.

II

IN THE MATTER OF:

UNITED STATES OF AMERICA v. JAMAL HASSIM, ET AL.,

TRIAL VOLUME 1

DAY ONE — MORNING SESSION

8:40 a.m.

Before: HON. WILLIAM T. MULLIGAN III.

District Judge

THE COURT

Ladies and Gentlemen of the jury, please give your undivided attention to Assistant United States District Attorney Patrick J. Fitzpatrick as he delivers his opening on behalf of the United States.

MR. FITZPATRICK

Good afternoon, members of the jury.

THE JURY

Good afternoon.

MR. FITZPATRICK

Bribes, kickbacks, fraud, and weapons of mass destruction. Plans to use the proceeds of financial crime to finance nationwide genocide on a scale that would surpass the carnage of 9/11 by tens of thousands — perhaps hundreds of thousands — of casualties. That's what you are going to learn about in this courtroom. Nearly two years ago, both of the defendants on trial were caught red-handed by a government informant, who, at risk to his own life, recorded the plotting and promoting of their criminal scheme to cheat honest investors, the U.S. AID program, and union members of this city out of money, so that they could pursue their dream of mass murder against our nation's most vulnerable, valuable, and precious resource: our children.

To achieve their dream of perpetrating the largest act of terrorism in the history of this country — in the history of the *world* — they needed money. They schemed to get their hands on the tens of millions of dollars such a wide ranging and ambitious operation required by setting up fraudulent "front companies" that appeared to be legitimate, but were, in fact, nothing more than recruiting vehicles for the murderous volunteers their multifaceted plot required and the financial sponsors needed to support them.

Their scheme centered on two companies, both domiciled on the Philippine island of Mindanao, known to harbor Islamic terrorists associated with Abu Sayyaf, a small terrorist group that has kidnapped and beheaded scores of people — including American missionary, Martin Burnham — and Jemaah Islamiyah, Al Qaeda's partner in Southeast Asia, best known for the bombing attacks on Bali nightclubs that killed more than two hundred people in 2002. It was groups of highly-trained enemy combatants like these, and others with a similar philosophy and agenda — like the Moro Liberation Front — that Jamal Hassim and Sheik Tarak Yousoff sought to support. They schemed to accomplish this goal by setting up businesses called Bangsamoro Seaweed and Aqua Venture, which on the surface looked lawful, but were, in fact, fraudulent stock deals that involved inflated, manipulated markets that would throw off millions of dollars in cash.

Now, the defendant's criminal plan, because it was so ambitious, didn't stop with crooked investment deals. It also set its sights on several union pension funds here in the New York City area. One of them, the proof will show, was run by members of the Gambino crime family. Another was the retirement fund that serves the interests of New York's finest, the detectives of the New York City Police Department.

This enterprise began back in 1995, when Jamal Hassim and Sheik Tarak Yousoff, along with others from Mr. Yousoff's mosque, created a fraudulent company called Bangsamoro Seaweed, which, the proof will show, engaged in stock fraud through insider trading between members of the Oulel-Albab Mosque, to raise profits and cheat unsuspecting public investors out of their money. The fraud at Bangsamoro Seaweed was going on for years before June 2006, when these defendants turned their attention toward the creation of another fraudulent company called Aqua Venture, and the pension funds of the working men and women of New York. The proof will show that they schemed to get their hands on this union pension money by offering bribes to union officials, which they planned to invest in the crooked Aqua Venture deal. You will learn that they planned to funnel the profits from this fraud into a shady offshore investment bank, which would allow them to secretly disburse this illegal money to arms dealers and poison manufacturers for the purchase of weapons of mass destruction that they planned to use against innocent children swimming in water parks and American civilians living near nuclear facilities.

You will learn that Aqua Venture and Bangsamoro Seaweed were conceived specifically to provide technical and financial support to armed Islamic insurgents in the Philippines, which led to yet another fraud that cheated American taxpayers out of tens of millions of dollars. This fraud targeted a program called USAID, which is sponsored by the U.S. government to help poor, underprivileged Muslims turn away from terror groups and re-immerse themselves in the community through the creation of honest, legitimate job opportunities. The fraud here is obvious. These defendants lied to officials in Washington to gain funds that would be used for the exact opposite purpose for which they were intended.

Seated in the third seat at the center table is Major Jamal Hassim, an honors student from the Air Force Academy, with sixteen years of service in the Air Force. Hassim had a flawless resume. Beyond impeccable, you will learn. These are the words that were used describe Major Hassim's record by a cooperating witness you will meet in this trial, who exposed Hassim's scheme just in the nick of time, before he was able to fully implement it.

You will learn that Jamal Hassim appeared to be the perfect patriot, which made him the perfect front man for this enterprise. He seemed like an all-American success story. But the proof will show that while Major Hassim was flying congressmen, senators, bombs, and artillery for the Air Force, he was living a sinister double life that included membership in Sheik Tarak Yousoff's mosque. The proof will show that the sheik, the gentleman in the fifth seat at the center table, is a known extremist, who once said the war in Iraq was, and I quote, "an act of baseless aggression." You will learn that the illegal activities engaged in by Major Hassim were inspired, to a large degree, by Sheik Yousoff's hateful, anti-American rhetoric. You see, Sheik Yousoff wanted to get even with the people of the United States for what he considered "an illegal war," by declaring a war of his own, which he planned to fight in pools, milk cartons, ketchup bottles, and soda pop cans. So he hatches a plan to finance this war with Jamal Hassim, by using illegal market manipulations to prop up the profits of two companies he secretly controlled with co-conspirators who were members of his mosque, who are not here on trial.

You will learn that one of the participants in this manipulation scheme was Conner Skilling, who was arrested for stock fraud in 1995. You will also learn that soon thereafter, Mr. Skilling began to cooperate secretly with the government. At the government's direction, Conner Skilling maintained his role as a corrupt investment banker, providing information to the FBI about ongoing stock scams on Wall Street.

Conner Skilling is what's known as a cooperating witness. He has since pled guilty to two crimes, and he hopes to receive a lenient sentence when he is ultimately sentenced. You will also learn that Mr. Skilling sometimes wore a recording device, usually in the area of his groin, to avoid detection from bad guys, like Mr. Hassim, whom he feared would kill him if they discovered he was a government informant.

Throughout this trial you will hear explicit, tape-recorded conversations that Mr. Skilling had with defendant Jamal Hassim, which were made at the direction of the FBI. You're going to hear, in explicit terms, plans being made to bribe union members and inflate manipulated markets. In tapes of private, intercepted conversations between Sheik Yousoff and Jamal Hassim, you will hear code words like "grouper," "bangus," and "blood cockle" used to disguise discussions about stock fraud and attack plans. You will also hear testimony from Conner Skilling and another witness about recorded conversations in which Jamal Hassim explicitly stated, "I believe in Ayatollah Khomeini's interpretation of the Koran; I believe it is the Muslim duty to defend Muslim interests against the Great Satan by all means possible." And "In my opinion Western policy has been consistently oppressive toward the Muslim community since the days of Saladin, which entitles Muslims, under Koranic law, to retaliate with whatever methods and weapons are available to them."

The means and the methods envisioned by those involved in this scheme included lacing food products with weaponized botulism which Dr. Ahn Hassim, Jamal Hassim's wife, planned to smuggle out of her lab at the Centers for Disease Control. The means and methods also included readiness drills through the use of laser tag, which Hassim played with members of his mosque, to train them in the use of force, which he and his co-conspirators anticipated might be necessary when they enacted their plan to hijack Air Force jets and overtake guards at the nuclear sites they planned to bomb. Finally, and most horribly, the means and methods included plans to pollute water at theme park swimming pools with cyanide, a deadly poison which easily permeates the skin, causing almost-instant death. The proof will show that the Hassims cased countless American water parks for at least two years with Sheik Tarak Yousoff and other conspirators, not presently on trial, to prepare for this horrific scheme.

Let me just say a few brief words about how the government investigated this case because an awful lot is going to be said in this trial about the government's cooperating witness, Conner Skilling, and his relationship with the FBI. There is going to be an awful lot said about his testimony, its significance, and what, if anything, it means with respect to what Jamal Hassim said on tape. Now, there is not going to be any dispute that Conner Skilling is a terrible person who committed serious crimes that cost investors millions of dollars.

You are going to learn of his agreement, that he pled guilty to two crimes in 1995, but that he hasn't been sentenced yet, and that he hopes to receive a more lenient sentence for assisting the government in this and other very dangerous operations. You will learn that Mr. Skilling is an asset of the FBI, and that he has been paid over a hundred thousand dollars a year in salary and expenses to maintain his undercover role as a wealthy investment banker. You're also going to learn that in return for assisting the government, that the government is allowed to tell the sentencing judge about his contribution to the justice system and that the judge can consider that in figuring his sentence.

You are going to learn that there were no upfront financial penalties to Skilling. He didn't have to pay money back in early 1995 when he signed this agreement. You will learn that the government permitted him to keep the money he had made illegally while he was cooperating, so that he could maintain his role as a corrupt investment banker and keep up a successful appearance to the charged enterprise. You are going to learn he has been a cooperating witness for a long time, and that there have been some problems with his cooperation.

You are going to learn, for example, that Skilling failed to file his tax returns for five years after he started cooperating and that not doing so was a violation of his agreement. You will hear that the government continued to use Conner Skilling in connection with its investigations anyway. You are also going to learn that Conner

Skilling filed a false affidavit in a civil lawsuit, a false statement under oath. As Judge Mulligan told you, you are the judges of the facts, and that includes the credibility of the witness. Conner Skilling's credibility is important, and we ask you to consider it carefully.

But, at the end of the day, we are confident that you are going to see Conner Skilling for exactly what he is — a tool that the FBI used to further important investigations essential to the protection of homeland security. You will see, more importantly, that that tape-recorded conversations Mr. Skilling had with Jamal Hassim capture fully — virtually fully — his dealings with Mr. Hassim and the broader conspiracy he represented.

The key issue in this trial is not whether Conner Skilling is a nice man, or whether the deal he made with the government could have been done differently. These issues are not on trial, though defense lawyers will surely bring these points out to distract you from the real issue, which is the state of mind of these defendants. That, we will prove to you, is fully revealed on the tapes of Jamal Hassim recorded by Conner Skilling. Additional proof of their state of mind will also be provided to you through tapes of private, coded conversations between Sheik Yousoff and Jamal Hassim, on which Mr. Skilling does not appear or have any influence, and tapes of Sheik Yousoff recorded by FBI agents attending services at the Oulel-Albab Mosque. The state of mind of both these defendants is fully revealed on these tapes, and you will see that nothing about Conner Skilling's relationship with the government has anything to do with what they were thinking, nor can it alter what's on the tapes. So in light of that, as criticism of the government's agreement with Skilling continues throughout this trial you should ask yourselves, why are we spending so much time on this?

I ask you, as we listen to these tapes together over the upcoming weeks, to use your common sense as you try to decide what the tapes mean, and remember that grown men, in unguarded conversations where they don't understand they're being taped, generally say what they mean.

Take their words at face value when they talk on these tapes.

Side A
8/08/08

Mr. Fitzpatrick! Welcome to my home away from home, or the regency suite, as we call it in the local dialect.

Let me show you into the sitting room while room service prepares our lunch.

Not for nothin', but I think you could have gotten me a better view.

Only joking.

I love the Statue of Liberty!

I even named a company after her.

What company was that?

Oh, some subsidiary — one of my endeavors from a long time ago.

While we're on the subject of old, you should tell Varlet over there it's time for a new suit. It's like I says to my boy Farrow the other day, "Since you guys have all the power, you might as well dress to kill!"

He didn't laugh either, but you know me, I can't resist a little quip.

Just so you know, I have a cute little place in Paramus, which I haven't been to in three years or five years, or whatever the case may be, but it's a real good shop. If you ever decide to stop cornering the market on black at the Men's Warehouse and finally step up to some Brioni, go there and ask for the owner.

His name is Moe.

He's a near and dear friend of mine.

A real knockaround guy.

Should you tell him I sent you?

That's a good one Fitzie.

You could go and do that.

I don't give a shit.

But don't be surprised if he tries tabbin' you up for my bill.

Let me grab the door for a minute, and sign for this food.

I ordered us a three hundred dollar smorgasbord.

I know, I know.

I have to be more careful, so your boss can't say, "Hey, why can't you control this guy? He spends five times his limit every week."

And you know what I say to that? I say, "You got to pay for quality." And besides, when you're spending twenty million dollars to prosecute a case, what's a few thousand more?

Do you really think anyone will notice?

Anyway, I did this for you. I figured that since you guys have been eating from the courthouse cafeteria all week, you could use some real food. We've got shrimp, lobster salad, some crab cakes, sliced steak — and for you Fitzie, a bottle of Mouton, to toast to your success.

And that's on me, not Uncle Sam, so you can't say no.

Court is adjourned until Monday, so hold up your flutes, boys, and let's salute Sheik Tarak Youssof, "The father of needy people!" Isn't that what he said in court today?

Okay, well I wasn't there, so you'll have tell me so I get it right.

He what?

Oh, even better!

He stood up and started screaming at the end of your opening? What did he say?

Wait. Wait. I can't understand you. You have to stop laughing.

Do it again Fitzie, do it again.

You're good.

You got his voice perfect.

Oh. I can just see him now in his white robe with that stupid silver sash, squealing like a stuck pig, "They are lying to you! God will punish them for their lies! They call me in Mindanao that I am the father of needy people!"

I love it!

Yeah, I agree.

That headline this morning helped to set it up.

It couldn't be better. I saw it myself when I had breakfast.

"NY to Qaeda Fly Boy: Fry."

That's the one, right?

I mean, they were all good, but that one was the best.

I'm sure that helped to flip his turban.

No doubt about the two years in solitary too.

Those concrete cubes at Manhattan Correctional definitely don't produce a calming effect. But the headline, I'm sure that's what put him over the top.

So tell me the truth, you set that up, right?

Oh, come on. We're all friends here, so there're no secrets, and anyway, who could I tell? I'm under round-the-clock protection in a room I can't leave twenty-four hours a day.

You got to give me some entertainments.

Vartie's smiling, so I know I'm on to something.

Come on. You're talkin' to me. We've buried a hundred and twenty three bodies together, and the count ain't all in yet.

You know that I know how to keep things quiet. So who was it?

The U.S. Attorney herself?

I'm surprised.

I mean, when you put it that way, I guess it makes eminent sense. She passes scoops and secrets, and they help her tip the scales.

It's a brilliant strategy.

In Brooklyn we call it one hand washing the other.

Hey, tell her if she ever decides to get into the stock promotion business, we'd make a great team.

Only kidding, only kidding.

But seriously, it puts all the players just where you want them. Like Judge Mulligan ain't gonna say no to any of your motions, 'cause he don't want to look like he's endangering the national security — and the defendants get all shook up, even the self-righteous ones, like our little major, which makes them look all nervous and guilty.

Vartie told me that you even got my boy Jamal Hassim looking spooked today.

You know what they say —

Once you start to thaw their confidence it melts away like paper equity.

You're right, especially if it's from one of my stocks!

Okay, okay, I'll get serious.

Let me put my glasses on and look at today's court order forensically for a few minutes, so we can start to do some prep.

All right, let's see:

```
————————————————x
UNITED STATES OF AMERICA
              -v-                    ORDER
JAMAL M. HASSIM, et al.,         S4 00 632 (WHP)
Defendants.
————————————————x
```

For the reasons stated on the record during conferences in this matter, it is hereby ordered that the defendant's motions concerning evidence is decided as follows:

Jamal M. Hassim:

Defendant Hassim's motion to preclude government testimony about potential risk of death to FBI investigators, including Conner Skilling, at the time of his arrest is denied.

Defendant Hassim's motion to preclude portions of a high security e-mail written by Conner Skilling, dated June 18, 2006, to the extent it concerns Mr. Skilling's stated recollection of unintelligible conversation is denied.

Defendant Hassim's motion to preclude files taken from

the computer of Ahn Hassim to the extent those files pertain to chemical weapons of mass destruction is denied.

Tarak J. Youssof:

Defendant Youssof's motion to preclude government exhibit 424 (GX 424), regarding his withdrawal of *Bin Laden: The Man Who Declared War on America*, from a public library in Alpharetta, Georgia, is denied.

Defendant Youssof's motion to preclude admission of videotaped images of Osama bin Laden is denied.

You fuckin' smoked 'em Fitzie!

This calls for another round.

I mean, you know, I'm gonna tell ya somethin'; I don't care what they can dig up about me and what they know. With this kind of ammo I can put my best shoe forward, like it don't matter.

So let them try to come knockin' me down after you just had their eyeteeth's removed. The welcome wagon's not gonna be out.

See what I'm tryin' to say?

I mean, you already got Judge Mulligan to put this jury under protection, which already's got these guys marked shit.

And this is their little claim to fame like, "I had to risk my life and serve anonymously, under cover, but I did it for the sake of my country."

You're laughing, but you know it's true.

That's how people think. They can swear under oath they're gonna be impartial all they want, but at the end of the day if they perceive a guy under twenty-four-hour surveillance in a high security cell is so dangerous that he can still be a threat to them personally, as we like to say in Brooklyn, the table is preset —

Our way —

With the only utensils being knives.

Then you finish them off with videos of bin Laden's greatest hits, some pictures of Ground Zero, a few theories about laser tag and stolen air force jets aimed at nuclear reactor sites and you got them stewing in their own juices, ready to tar Hassim and his sheik with the brush of iniquity.

That's my Sigmund Freud analysis.

What do you mean I left out the best part?

What other part is there?

No, I'm serious, Vartie didn't tell me nothin' except the jury was sent home early with court being canceled for the afternoon having to do with some kind of beef between you and the defense — but I got no clue why. I guess he wanted you to give me the news yourself.

You finally worked out a plea deal with Malik?

Hey, congratulations!

Let me guess, he's gonna testify that Jamal Hassim tried to recruit him off-tape to become a member of Al Qaeda.

And help the wife mix botulism into lunches to be served at various public schools?

You're the fuckin' best!

That explains why we're munching on filet in the middle of the afternoon.

You fuckin' knocked old Brandy over the head with a two-by-four, and he asked for a delay so he could assess the damage.

I got to hand it to ya Fitzie, you're pretty smooth for a guy who looks like he still dips his Oreos in milk.

And it's a one-two punch, 'cause them supporters on the court-house steps won't wanna be seen wavin' pictures of Ahn Hassim no more, talkin' up her record of tolerance and peace.

They'll be scattering quicker than buckshot, sayin', "Appearances are so deceiving. We were fooled by a terrorist, 'cause she played her part so innocent and sweet."

And it couldn't be better, 'cause now that you got them on the defensive, the public won't care where you got her hidden and what kind of interrogation you do.

They'll be like, "We just want to know the truth, however you got to get it," as in, "We don't need to know all the dirty details, 'cause you're workin' for our safety, so we're puttin' our support behind you."

Sometimes ya gotta to shake things up like that to give yourself a clean shot at the other side.

As I've been known to so cleverly say, "There's nothin' like a lit-tle stinger in the morning, to shoot their equilibrium out of the sky."

Now you know what it feels like to be Barry Bonds hittin' a drive into McCovey Cove, even if he had to do it on a little bit of a cheat.

That's why I'm about to crack the cork on this Latour '82.

Oh, no, no, no.
Don't give me that bullshit anything can still happen.
Yeah, right.
And if the queen had balls she'd be king.
Salute!

I know, I know.
We have to work on a position con-conjunctively about the kava

so we can create a story we can work with. Let me just fill my plate here with some of this Dungeness crab, and settle myself down.

Okay.

So you think they're gonna say I purposely disabled Hassim by repeatedly badgering him to drink a substance that contains narcotic properties.

And I'm gonna say — *we're* gonna say — that Hassim drank kava of his own free will, and that there's no evidence that it has any narcotic effect...never been identified by the DEA as a controlled substance, sold over the Internet and in health food stores...blah, blah, blah.

All right.

And when they say there's a mountain of evidence that a half-ounce of kava has the same narcotic effect as a 10-milligram Valium, you're gonna say even if it could be proved, arguendo, that kava could likely have some mild narcotic effect on certain users, the strength of that effect on Hassim, if there was any at all, can't be testified to, since the kava he drank was homemade. Any testimony about its strength and possible effect would be mere conjecture, and unfairly prejudicial to the government.

Yackity, yackity, yackity.

Okay. Got it.

Looks like we got 'em boxed in on this one.

Not completely?

What's the problem?

Hassim can be heard complaining of a headache and sensitivity to light in tape 2D? So what?

Okay, so they'll argue those are two signs of kava intoxication; and we'll argue those are two signs of being tired, which, I happen to know from personal experience, Hassim was. So they got no proofs.

They say they do?

How's that?

An interpreter of Bislama inspected the transcripts?

I didn't even know there was such a thing.

Who the fuck interprets Melanesian Pig Latin?

The schmuck who writes the authoritative dictionary on it — of course.

That makes sense.

And he says what?

When I'm ordering a cup of kava for Hassim at the kava bar in tape 2C, I'm saying, "Excuse me partner, two shells please, kava, extra strong."

Hmm. Let me take a look at the printout of that.

Well, I have to tell you that I don't agree. I remember that night very clearly, and when I said, "Excuse me partner, two shells please, *kava we I nokaot*," what I was saying was, "Excuse me partner, two shells please, kava, extra light, for beginners."

And I'll swear to that.

No, no.

I understand we have to overcome this, 'cause right after the kava bar I start having my little conversation about Hassim's interpretation of Islam and holy war, and it doesn't look good if I got him stoned first.

So I'll testify I didn't.

It's my word against his — and he's a fuckin' terrorist.

Then all that's left is that little quip where I say, "*Waiter! Laetum out. Tispun man I save drong kwik.*" Right?

Okay, so they interpret that as what?

"Waiter, lights down for the cheap drunk."

Well I have an entirely different interpretation. What I'm gonna say I said is, "Waiter, lights down, it's too bright in here."

Their expert can argue all he wants that the word "tispun" means "drunk" in Bislama. I'll say it means "tired" in the dialect spoken in my neighborhood.

You'll just get a professional interpreter from the FBI to confirm that.

See, the thing I don't understand is why any of this is important.

Didn't Judge Mulligan rule that none of the statements I make on tape are being admitted for the truth of the matter anyways, that they're just used as a probe, to reveal state of mind?

That's my point, since your position is that the government has the right to allow informants to exaggerate the facts, why can't we just say I was exaggerating about Hassie being drunk, or overstating his condition a little bit?

And I'm sure now that you've got Malik on board you won't need too much coaxing to get him to back me up.

Like he could say, "That's Conner, always joking. I was with Hassim that whole night when those tapes were recorded, and he was straight as straw."

And you won't have to take no risks with him.

Just ask him one of your cute little questions like, "Jamal Hassim wasn't drunk that night you and Conner took him out to eat at Rossi's, *right?*" and he'll catch your meaning like my German Shepherd catches a twenty-ounce strip.

Okay, okay.

We'll opt for plan A, if that's what you think is best.

It's your playbook.

I'm just the tool.

So let me take a listen to those unintelligibles you wanted me to review, and put them through the spin cycle again...

IN THE MATTER OF:

UNITED STATES OF AMERICA v.
JAMAL HASSIM, ET AL.,

TRIAL VOLUME 2
DAY TWO – MORNING SESSION
8:30 a.m.

(Trial resumed)
(Jury not present)

THE COURT

I hope you have a good reason for keeping us all waiting, Mr.
Brand.

MR. BRAND

I do, your Honor. Last evening I spent time going through the government's latest transcripts, which were provided to my office late
yesterday afternoon. When I compared them to previous "final
transcripts" the government provided to the defense, it became
apparent that the government has made additional, unannounced
changes in terms of words spoken, even now, after the trial has
begun.

For instance, in the newest final translation of tape 2D, there is an
attribution that has Mr. Hassim saying, "I really have a good understanding of the Koran, to make these Muslims who want peace
understand there is no choice but war." This is a radical change
from text in the final transcripts the government provided us just two
weeks ago. In that version, this same passage reads as follows: "I
really have a good understanding of the Koran, which I intend to use

to make these Muslims who want peace understand alternatives to war."

Judge, the government's original draft transcript of the same snippet of conversation, produced a year ago, has Mr. Hassim saying, in the same portion of tape, "I really have (UI, or unintelligible) to make these (UI)."

We maintain that this original interpretation, which conforms to their witness's own version of the conversation heard on this tape as he represented it in an e-mail sent to the FBI right after it was recorded — when his recollection of events would have arguably been the strongest — is the only reliably accurate representation of this piece of conversation, since this part of the tape is almost completely inaudible.

MR. VARLET

The changes Mr. Brand is complaining about in 2D concern a snippet of dialogue Mr. Brand urged the government to reconsider concerning the accuracy of our transcript. He particularly wanted a change in the line on page 30 about Mr. Hassim's stated understanding of the Koran as it pertains to holy war. In order to accommodate his concern, we had Mr. Skilling go back and listen to the tape again, and he heard more. It's not our fault he didn't hear what Mr. Brand wanted him to hear, and that in the process of going through this, in the midst of a great deal of litigation about the accuracy of the transcripts on the part of the defense, he heard some things differently. Mr. Skilling made changes to the transcript in the pursuit of the most accurate transcript he could make, which we then we turned over to the defense.

THE COURT

Mr. Brand, Mr. Skilling was the primary agent for the government in this investigation, and as such, is viewed as the most reliable source to interpret the tapes he made. You may disagree with his version of events, but the government is perfectly within its rights to allow him to reconstruct conversations that may be somewhat unclear.

MR. BRAND

What is unclear to me is when this process of reinterpretation ends. When is a final transcript final? If you compare the final transcripts from two weeks ago with the final version we're using today, you'll notice that in addition to countless word changes, more dialogue has been edited out as well. The government has cut out whole portions from dialogue they previously told us they were going to play, like this, recorded right before Conner Skilling asks a question about holy war:

> CS: I keep telling this boy he's got to loosen up.
> MT: He looks plenty loose to me.
> CS: Oh, he ain't anywhere near your loose-o-meter. He's straight as a pool stick, aren't ya kid?
> Waiter: Excuse me sir, may I fill you up again?
> CS: By all means. Hey, Jamal, don't cover up your shell.

I could go on and cite other changes the government made to their final transcripts, but after spending several hours going through them, I still don't know what they are, since I didn't get this latest edition until yesterday, while I was meeting with my client, trying to decipher new FBI 501 material concerning Malik el-Tiberius, which was sprung on us less than forty-eight hours ago. The only fair remedy the defense is left with, your Honor, is to ask for another delay.

THE COURT

I said on Friday there could be no more delays.

MR. BRAND

Yes, and you also said there should be no more surprises.

THE COURT

At the break, the government is to provide defense counsel with a list of textual changes they made to various statements they are playing.

MR. VARLET

Yes, your Honor. I think there may be a way for us to produce that material to them, and we will attempt to do that. I would like to say, your Honor, that we sought permission from your Honor, and received it, to make typographical and fine-tuning changes of this nature, right up to the time of trial, which of course makes eminent sense, since the goal is to have as accurate a transcript as possible.

THE COURT

I don't think the defendants are arguing with that. I'm certainly not. I think their concern is knowing what changes were made, without having to sit two lawyers in a room, reading transcripts to each other to see where they have been changed.

MR. VARLET

I think we have some material we can distribute that ought to capture most of the latest adjustments. I can't guarantee information on all of the changes, but almost all of them. We'll get that under way at noontime today.

THE COURT

If there are no other matters, I will bring in the jury, and let Mr. Brand begin his opening statement.

HEADLINE NEWS
12:32 ET

DEFENSE MAKES OPENING STATEMENT FOR QAEDA AIR MAN

>>Donald Brand, lawyer for defendant Jamal Hassim, the decorated Air Force major accused of treason, terrorism, and stock fraud delivered his opening statement this morning to a skeptical jury, amidst accusations by the prosecution of professional misconduct and misrepresentation of the facts. After a heated exchange between the government and the defense about the admissibility of defense claims concerning the conduct of the government witness in this case — whose identity remains a secret outside the courtroom for security reasons — the presiding federal district court judge, William Mulligan, allowed defense attorneys to argue that it was the witness himself, not the accused men, who should be on trial.

>>Can you tell us the basis for these claims?

>>According to his defense lawyer, the government witness used Mr. Hassim as a "human shield" to draw attention away from his own illegal activities, which, according to the defense, can be heard on redacted portions of FBI tapes the government has chosen not to

play at trial, a charge prosecutors strongly deny.

>>What was the nature of the illegal activity that the witness allegedly engaged in?

>>Most of the allegations by the defense against the witness center around stock manipulation. Apparently, this witness has been involved in a number of "pump and dump" stock swindles over the years, where the price of a stock is artificially "pumped up" and secretly sold off, or "dumped," ahead of public trading.

>>What does this have to do with terrorism?

>> The defense maintains that this is a witness with his own agenda, who should not be trusted. Donald Brand, Mr. Hassim's attorney, claimed in his opening that Mr. Hassim called FBI headquarters in Washington just hours before his arrest two years ago. The defense says this call was made to report a proposal by the government witness for Mr. Hassim to sell portable anti-aircraft missiles, known as Manpads, to members of the Muslim militia groups Mr. Hassim had contact with in the Philippines. The FBI denies ever receiving such a call.

>>What was the jury's reaction?

>>I have to say that they remained largely impassive throughout most of Mr. Brand's presentation. I did notice a few jurors exchanging dubious glances when Mr. Brand talked about the alleged Manpad deal. One of them, I think it was juror number eight, openly laughed at this defense allegation. Overall, I don't think this strategy worked.

Side B
8/26/08

Hey Fitzie! Top of the afternoon to ya!

If Inga didn't have such good hands, I'd let you take my place on the table. I'm sure she'll stay if you want an hour.

Right hon?

And she's a really friendly girl. If you want some aromatherapy, she can rub you down with lavender for your stress or put gravy on your turkey in some other way.

You know me, I'm a full service provider.

Just call me Deep Tissue.

Oh don't look so sour, I'm just making a humorous, glib comment.

Hey, you were the one who told me I had to stay laid low.

I figured since I'm reasonably unfettered from great scrutiny right now, I'd let Inga help me follow your instructions...but if you want to have a "holier than thou" attitude, which you and I know is something of a smoke screen, I'm gonna ask, "Who are you? Father Flanagan?"

And before you answer, "yes" don't forget who butters your breads.

See, Inga, when you hang around with us you automatically become a team player, except when my esteemed associate here needs to take care of something very quiet.

Then we got to throw you out of the huddle.

Let me close the door so no one can hear.

There.

Now you can tell me what's wrong.

As I always say, I'd rather be on the receiving end, personally.

It's like I always tell Farrow, you got to monitor a situation closely, 'cause information is power, and if you don't do that, you could end up with your dick in your hands.

That's the position Farrow's in now?

Well, that can't be a good thing being that his is about the size of a gherkin.

And you're saying that's my fault?

How's that?

Look, I made this case for him.

His involvement in the development of this story makes the Maytag repairman look busy.

Not for nothin' but when you hire some stumblebum out of a law school from the bottom of the pickle barrel who wants the job, 'cause he can't even chase ambulances right, you ain't gonna get an Academy performance.

So Brandy's knocking him around a bit.

Okay, humbling him and making him look like a fool, because he had to admit I was involved with Myers Shellac while I was taping Hassim, and running a few stocks I shouldn't have.

But you knew about that.

I can't believe you didn't have him better prepared.

I understand you can't prepare him about stuff you don't have any knowledge of.

As far as I know I've been completely forthright.

What did I miss?

Okay, the seven hundred and fifty thousand dollar tax lien I skipped out on three years ago when I sold the farm in Jersey due to filing late returns.

That was just an oversight.

The millions Candy made last year from manipulated equities?

You know what they say Fitzie, the husband is always the last to know.

A short position in Bangsamoro Seaweed run through a brokerage firm in Indonesia?

I don't know anything about that.

It certainly wasn't done in *my* name.

And a stock called Merrico?

Pumped and popped right after Hassim was arrested?

You won't find *me* on *that* investor list.

How would I know Rodney Flitch was on the board?

Or one of the largest shareholders?

That's news to me.

I'll deny having anything to do with that, I don't care what they have on tape.

I was just introducing what I thought were two legitimate operators.

What they did with that stock between themselves isn't my business.

Oh, you want to play bad cop with me?

If it makes you feel official to read that happy horseshit, knock yourself out.

Attorney General's Guidelines on **FBI** Use of Informants and Confidential Sources: Clause E:


```
"Each such person shall be advised that his relationship
```

with the FBI will not protect him from arrest or prosecution for any violation of Federal, State, or local law, except where the FBI has determined pursuant to these guidelines that his association in a specific activity, which otherwise would be criminal, is justified by law enforcement."

So what's the problem?

There's plenty of plausible justification for my activities.

How was I supposed to play my part without a bankroll?

I didn't notice the Justice Department offering to pay my mortgage, or the lease on my Mercedes, or to foot the bill for my vacations or my rent.

What I mean is, when I'm posing as a rich investment banker and people I'm investigating for the FBI pop into New York or Vanuatu or Sydney or wherever, they have to be entertained appropriately, and coddled and made to feel important. That's how you do business, and if we're gonna be good at that, somebody's gotta pay. So if I gotta spend, ya know, five, six G's to let a guy run amuck, that's just the cost of doin' business.

It gives me a cloak of tremendous credibility, and puts some sizzle on my plate.

Like with Hassie.

That was the best five grand we ever spent, so don't sit here and tell me about the lousy salary of a hundred thousand you pay me, or the twenty million you let me keep ten years ago.

Who do I look like, Santa Claus?

And don't start talking like, "Don't ask, don't tell means don't know."

Let's not mince words, you and Farrow don't ask no questions, like, "What are they doing over there, Conner and Rod?" because these are topics you don't want discussed in front of you 'cause then you would be put in a very, very compromising, awkward position.

You don't wanna ever be in that position.

See, I'll go naked in the steam bath for you.

I ain't bashful.

It don't matter, I could give a shit about that.

I'm just watching your back, and segregating your interests.

Listen, every once in a while we're gonna run into someone who has a cube root of a brain, but we can still play ten steps ahead. Especially with your guys tapped into all of Hassie's movements, twenty-four hours a day.

So don't sit there and tell me that I wrecked your chances 'cause I made a couple of little slips.

You know there ain't a market I can't trade if I get advance scoop.

And it's worked out splendidly, like when you told me about your guys overhearing Brandy's preparations for questions on the little mistakes I made in my e-mails and such. It gave me time to pre-prepare the bob and weave without having to rush when he said, "Why the in vitro story when your wife had a hysterectomy ten years back?"

And you heard me when I answered, "Sir, you misconstrue a philosophical discussion about crime taking root in a fertile valley, stated in a very cordial manner. It's unseemly to overly pontificate when you're tryin' to stop terrorists from launching a deadly attack."

After that, no one cared when Brandy went into that sideline on how I was taking your eye off the ball through the use of personal schmooze — which of course, I would never do.

And it worked out wonderfully, 'cause it got the jurors deadly focused back on Hassie, and the tactics he was planning to use.

Which is why I always told my brokers, "Make a special offer if you have to or whatever largesse, 'cause how you navigate the blippies will determine your success."

So, you'll have to be the judge of this, 'cause I don't wanna tell you how to conduct your theory, but perhaps consideration could be given to the idea that Rodney was conducting top-secret research undercover, as a subcontracting spy — which is why Farrow had to say, "I don't know" and " I can't recall" under cross-examination a hundred and twenty seven times.

When you get him on re-cross he can say he had no choice, 'cause it's an ongoing international investigation, with implications worldwide.

And it works out perfectly, 'cause it was too sensitive for him to make a decision while he was on the stand whether to say this or that, especially since Rod is such a high profile person and all. He can say, "I had to ask my supervisor first, 'cause this kind of revelation could cause the whole operation to collapse."

So this is one potential prop-proposition I can think of right on the fly.

As we like to say in Brooklyn, "When you're down to your last two dollars, make sure you spend 'em on a good shoeshine."

Come on. You never heard that?
Not for nothin', but ya gotta admit, its sorta a plum.
And a way of making Farrow gettin' caught flat-foot appear like a quality delay, instead of him just bein' dumb.

And Rod's analysis on this issue is likely gonna be my analysis as conveyed to him by me. And it couldn't be better, 'cause Rod's the kinda guy that knows how to sit down and play the piano like a virtuoso after just a few tries.

Meaning, we can have him dispatched on this issue in less time than it takes for a little bad news to cause the price of crude to spike.

So he'll put out a release through HIG, saying he was working with the FBI in the interest of global security.

It's great publicity for him, and a good juggle for you.

And think of this — when Brandy hears about another witness comin' out of the woodwork, his whole case will go completely off-kilter.

You're laughin' 'cause you know I'm right.

And the best part is we can say their tactics forced us to make disclosures against the best interests of the homeland...and global interests too.

You can say, "We were forced to compromise ethics and public security because of the way the defense chose to play."

And it's a great switch-up, 'cause Rod will look like the hero.

Brandy will likely be tellin' Hassie to take a deal for fifty years.

Merrico will disappear from discussion.

And this trial will go away. That makes this a win-win for everyone, as I would so eloquently say.

You like that, huh?

It's smooth but most aggressive.

That should make them feel a little uncomfortable and ameliorate the blip. They'll leave with their tails between their legs with us.

Trust me on this.

And to answer your question — you don't have to worry about anything else hockin' up on me.

As we're so fond of saying in Brooklyn — all the shit there is has already rolled downhill.

Which is good, 'cause it happened at the beginning of the trial.

Three months down the road, when it's time to vote for conviction, the knuckleheads you have on the jury will have forgotten that Farrow looked like a monkey today, or that I looked like a problem child.

There's no question about it, because I know the animals we're dealing with.

After they hear from Rod and Malik, they'll give you a vote of "guilty" on the whole prix fixe.

AUSTRALIAN FINANCIER ANNOUNCES
HIS ROLE WITH THE FBI

Member of Australia's In Crowd Reveals Undercover Role

SYDNEY, Australia, August 28 — Rodney Flitch, scion of one of Australia's wealthiest families and director of Humanity Insurance Group (HIG Insurance, Ltd.), announced early today that he has been working with American agents involved in the investigation of Jamal M. Hassim, the U.S. fighter pilot currently on trial for terrorism in New York. Though a statement released through HIG corporate headquarters acknowledged his involvement in the case, it leaves his exact role, and the timing of it, unclear. The tersely worded announcement states that "Mr. Flitch alerted American authorities about Mr. Hassim's suspicious behavior some time after meeting him at a promotional function held in Sydney for Aqua Venture LLC," a business venture organized by Mr. Hassim that American prosecutors allege was an elaborate fraud, designed to provide material support for terror organizations in the United States and the Philippines. Assistant U.S. District Attorney Jason Varlet confirmed that Mr. Flitch's name currently appears on the witness list, but added, "It's too early to predict if Mr. Flitch will be required to testify at the trial" of Mr. Hassim and co-defendant Sheik Tarak Youssof, which is anticipated to last at least another twelve weeks.

Side B
9/03/08

Oh come on, stop whinin' like a gelding. We've already figured out the roadmap to control this very intelligently.

What else could get in our way?

The Colonel Commander of the 89th Air Wing?

What's he got to do with this?

Well, everybody lists a few character witnesses, but you're good at scarin' 'em away.

Okay, so Hassie was popular amongst the ranks.

I don't care how many pilots in the Air Force liked this guy, when push comes to shove, they're not gonna like him so much that they'll be willing to put their careers on the line.

There were twenty-six willing to say good for him?

So you'll give them friendly reminders that they could be charged with dereliction of duty or possible collusion for lettin' suspicious behavior go on without filing a report. That's the key to the kingdom, and you know how to flip that switch. Anyways, Vartie told me you thinned the market by sixteen already. Is that right?

Okay, good. So it sounds like a prearranged thing.

And you'll get the rest of the crumbs to drop off that cake when you start ridin' herd over the next couple of weeks.

But that won't work with Colonel May?

You're sure, 'cause he said he'll have a sit down with some big-wigs in Washington who he happens to know on a first-name basis if you threaten him again?

Okay.

So it sounds like you switched out of it in a very crafty manner, from a PC point of view.

Makin' like he got it all wrong.

Like you were just worried about his exposure — wanting him to know what could happen. Not from you — 'cause you would never do that — but from somewhere else in the woodpile.

That was very stealthful of you Fitzie.

Listen, my feeling is he'll come around after this situation acquires another layer of maturity. You, know, like when some esteemed colleague from the Air War College calls him in for a little chat. If not, you can always apply alternative pressure, like we did with Rashid Dukes.

Remember at the debriefing, when he told Farrow it's common practice for Air Force pilots to take pictures of various military air-craft, and do target practice with laser guns?

God, were you freaked out.

And I was just sittin' back and laughin' at you and Vartie, getting your noses all bent outta shape.

When you were sayin', "We can't let this get out, 'cause it's a proof of our theory. If the jury hears, it could spoil the strength of our case."

You was both in panic — especially you Fitzie.

Which is why I finally said, "Why not go for a shot in the arm?"

I mean, I'm reactive — you're the planner.

But, let's face it, that strategy helped you create a profitable situation out of something that was going subpar.

And you seen from him what a meat scrap can give.

After you mentioned the possible promotion suddenly all that high-road shit about Hassie and his wife bein' Mr. and Mrs. "global peace" melted faster than an ice cream cone in Cancun.

Now there's speculation, geographically speaking, on what was his real purpose, flyin' in and out of all them down range airstrips in Baghdad and Kabul.

Was he smugglin' opium?

Or picking up messages from members of Al Qaeda?

Just what was he doin' during his leave time off base?

And that bit he did on gettin' ready to flag Hassie for suspicious activity just before the FBI came in — I'll tell ya, that was the best.

You know, when he said, "I knew as soon Agent Brown introduced himself, it had to be about Jamal Hassim. Because I was beginning to suspect him myself by that time..."

That put the icing on the cake.

And it worked out even better than expected, since he knew Hassie on a friends and family basis.

I mean, this guy was great!

My favorite was his interpretation of what Ahn Hassim might have meant when she said, "Take the whole family and have a blast," while she was organizing them congregational trips to theme parks and pools, which, upon further reflection, he now thinks might have been some clandestine signal for an imminent bombing, or possibly a series of chemical attacks.

And I'm sure he'll remember more collegial remarks about possible jihad-related activities when you get him on the stand.

Like, what might have been the entendre when Hassie told him he liked to "participate in tourism," while he was stationed in Qatar.

And all them instant messages about "opening new markets" with "nice brothers."

He'll spin that out for you in a very convincing manner — especially now that he's a Brigadier General.

What does he give a fuck?

Which is why I always told my brokers, "If the other side drives a hard bargain, you gotta put your balls up."

Oh, oh.

Now I understand the problem.

That won't work with May 'cause he's AARP.

Okay.

But that still don't answer why he's obstructing —

Well, when you put it like that, I suppose it's not hard to understand.

The 89th airlift squadron being the top secret and all, with missionized cabins, missile defense systems, secure voice and data communication, doing secret missions on an international basis.

So having a chief pilot who's plotting to blow up nuclear silos and poison water parks could be a little rough for his reputation on the national security side.

Especially when it was the Colonel himself who hired Hassie after three days of interviews.

Shit —

Then introduced him to his wife...

Listen, I agree.

It don't look good havin' some guy with a chest full of medals testifying that Jamal Hassim was a model citizen by everyone's standards until he ran into me.

That could wobble our story a little — even after you point out that Hassie's been retired from the 89th for over four years.

But you know what I always say, and we've chatted about this before —

There ain't nobody that doesn't have somethin' to hide.

Who knows what will come out when you put your stick in *his* beehive?

Vartie says you already wrote him up with some of them national security letters.

Which, let's face it, is basically a supermarket sweeps. Shit, now that you got that goin' your gonna know what this guy eats for breakfast in less than a week.

And it couldn't be easier.

I mean, alls you need to say is you got "reasonable suspicion" to give yourself carte blanche to look at anything you want. It ain't like you need a judge's signature or a warrant or nothin'.

Fuck, the FBI manufactures these things off the lint of a tennis ball.

Alls I'm saying is you need to weasel around, and do a little more due diligence.

Trust me, that's the way you'll find the nugget that leads to the vein.

Check his driving record, the web sites he visits — if he pays his taxes on time. Maybe you find out he has a fetish for phone sex. Or he's got some boy toy on the side.

One thing's for sure. There's something lurking in his background we can use to blow up his holier-than-thou image like a thermonuclear fucking landmine.

There's gotta be. There's gotta be.

I mean, the man's sixty-five.

Hey, remember when I first met you in your office on Center Street, when you made that remark about the yellow pages?

When you said, "Close your eyes, and let your finger drop wherever."

After all these years, I still can't get that guy outta my head.

I even remember the address:

872 Bayshore Drive

Massapequa, New York

Which, by the way, is where he still lives.

I know, cause I looked.

The point I'm tryin' to make is what you told me after I did that, after I picked out his name.

You have a good memory Fitzie.

That's exactly right.

You said, "Give me three months, and I'll be ready to indict."

Hold on to that thought while you're getting ready to retire our Colonel Commander for a second time.

And remember what you told me when I fingered Harry Bickler that day:

"Everybody's guilty of something."

SECRET

U.S. Department of Justice
Federal Bureau of Investigation

Southern District Field Division
One Saint Andrews Plaza
New York, New York 10007

Mr. John Sullivan
President
Information Guard
6710 Milwaukee Ave.
Milwaukee, Wisconsin

Dear Mr. Sullivan:

Under the authority of the Executive Order 12333, dated
December 4, 1981, and pursuant to Title 18, United States
Code (U.S.C.), Section 2709 (as amended, October 26, 2001),
you are hereby directed to provide the Federal Bureau of
Investigation with all information pertaining to the credit
history of Kenneth R. May, including third party information
you have access to from banks, telephone companies, and
Internet providers that will give a clear and exigent profile
of his personal activity.

In accordance with Title 18, U.S.C., Section 2709 (b), I
certify that the information sought is relevant to an authorized investigation to protect against international terror-

ism or clandestine intelligence activities, and that such an investigation of a United States citizen is not conducted solely on the basis of activities protected by the first amendment of the Constitution of the United States.

You are further advised that Title 18, U.S.C., Section 2709, prohibits any officer, employee or agent of yours from disclosing to any person that the FBI has sought or obtained access to information or records under these provisions.

Your immediate cooperation in this matter is greatly appreciated.

> Robert J. Kim
> Assistant Director/
> Special Agent in Charge

Side A
9/18/08

Okay, okay. I'll try to tone it down.

I'm wearin' the Swatch instead of my Rolex. How much more low-key do you want me to get? I already got a contact rash from the band. So I says to Farrow when we got back to the hotel, I says, "You got to go downstairs to the gift shop and get me some cortisone 'cause by tomorrow I'll have blisters."

When your skin's used to eighteen carat, wearing plastic is a shock. You'll see what I mean when you go out and get hired for seven figures at some white shoe joint like Hafflemeyer and Grey, or something like that, after you get famous for putting Hassie away.

Hey, I can't help it if my suits ain't tailored by Helen Keller.

No, and it isn't sharkskin.

Not for nothin', but haven't you ever heard of Dupioni silk?

All right, all right. I'll go back to wearin' a lighter color tomorrow.

No black.

No more grey.

Nothing that shines.

And a tie that's a little less colorful.

I know, I know.

We gotta sell an image here.

We can't have me lookin' sharp in three thousand dollar getups with Hassie sitting there all pathetic in his Air Force uniform with the medals stripped off.

Makes him look like too much of a victim.

Yeah, I know, especially with his father wearin' the same shaggy stuff every day, with all that publicity swirlin' about him sellin' his dry cleaner and mortgaging his bungalow in some slum outside Chicago to pay for the lawyers to save his only son.

It don't look good when I come struttin' in lookin' GQ when you got a situation like that, I agree.

You gotta be sensitive to appearances.

I just got sick of wearin' that tweed and khaki you had me in, but I'll go back to that tomorrow if you think it'll help.

Hey, I got an idea.

How about I wear one of those flag pins you guys got?

Or that tie with the flying nooses Candy bought you when you was waitin' for the verdict on the Suarez trial, 'cause that's what they're gonna put around Hassie's neck, especially after my testimony today.

I ain't tryin to toot my own horn or nothin', but you got to admit I held up like a iron man when Brandy was puttin' it to me about the breakaway conversations I had with Hassie right before you guys swooped in for the arrest.

Remember when he stared me down and said, "You just made that up, didn't you?"

You know, when he was asking questions about Hassie tellin' me how he couldn't wait to put a hurt on the operation of the Run Away River 'cause he thought Six Flags gypped him on the season pass, when he says to me, "The Cyclone should have been ready this year, like they promised. There's a lot of people gonna pay for that."

And when Brandy was up there tryin' to get all indignant and suggest I was lyin', you heard me, it was masterful when I said, "Mr. Brand, I could not sit idly by when freedom was about to be assaulted. Even though I didn't have a tape running at the time, 'cause at that point I was afraid — not for my own safety — I'm willing to make any sacrifice for my country — but for the well-being of my wife. And even though I was scared stiff of what they might do to her if they found out I was trying to foil their plot, I vowed to remember every word, so that I could assure freedom's victory."

Remember that?

And then I got that little tear goin' in my eye.

I'll tell you what, right after that, I slipped a peek over at juror number eight, while Brandy was contemplating his next move, and I saw it on her face.

You know, that look they get when they go hard, even though the judge keeps telling them, "Keep an open mind," and all that other happy horseshit.

But I saw it.

That tight little smile they give you to let you know they're on your side.

I'm telling ya Fitzie, she had it.

I had the buy ticket written.

I could have banked her on fifty thousand shares.

And you saw how I put the wood to Brandy with that.

He couldn't even come up for air.

Are you serious?

You think he didn't ask any follow up questions because I sounded so ridiculous he wanted the absurdity of my answer to hang in the room and resonate?

Well, that's your opinion.

I don't think I sounded smart alecky and false.

I think I sounded very official.

Yeah, yeah.

I remember what you said when we were doing Stockgate, about how my little offhand routines helped us lose the Gorstein trial.

Not for nothin', Fitzie, but one loss out of a hundred ain't bad.

I understand there's much more at stake here than goin' after some old man tryin' to raise money for a business that nobody knows nothin' about, 'cause he's just some anonymous septuagenarian outta Ridgefield tryin' to fund some ridiculous cockeyed dream about a fleet of commuter boats.

Those are the ones that don't hurt you too bad if they slip away.

Like, there ain't no apologies needed. Just, "Get the fuck outta here, and don't think because you were acquitted don't mean you weren't guilty, and that we won't be back at you again if you try to kick up any dust. So don't complain. Just swallow your losses and retire to the old-age home or wherever they send old broke-down Jews and thank your lucky stars you didn't end up chained down to one of them prison hospital beds."

This is a different case, I agree.

We got particular entertainment corporations with negative earning reports.

We got kids afraid to drink Coca-Cola.

The sales of milk are down.

We got the Air Force re-assigning all their camel jockeys, and Marines fanning through the jungles of Mindanao.

The reaction just went off the meter.

It's like I said to Farrow the last week when we were sitting around watchin' Oprah, waitin' for my turn to come up.

I says, "We gotta win this thing, 'cause if we don't all those book deals are fucked."

See, I've been spinnin' on this one, and I figure we can sell this as the most important case of espionage in U.S. history since the Rosenberg trial. And you know how people love stories about shady characters that are favorably inclined to do the right thing when the chips are down. Like in all those books about born-agains and rehabs and unlikely heroes and whatnot.

So I figure I look good for this, and I says to Candy, "When this is all done I'm gonna find us an agent," and I ain't talking about one like Farrow, who don't know a casting grid from a parking grid.

I'm talking about farmin' this out to the real deal.

You know, a guy with an office off Wilshire Boulevard who really understands how to sell a concept.

Okay, I understand.

I hit a little bit of a bad streak today, and I got to dial it down.

You got my word.

No more long answers. No more sermonizing. No speculation.

Just a naked "no" or "yes."

"I don't remember."

"Can you repeat that again?"

"I don't recall."

"I need to refresh my memory."

The standard stuff.

I know the script.

Focus on what I already said to the FBI in the 501 reports.

Don't add no more new information until it's time for re-cross, and only after I review it with you.

I understand.

We got to figure this like a custom tailor, like a made-to-measure suit. We need to take the measurement before we know what we're capable of doing.

You can count on me.

I'm a professional.

If I have to answer thirty questions, I'm gonna know the answer to five hundred questions, 'cause I never get short and surprised.

IN THE MATTER OF

UNITED STATES OF AMERICA v.
JAMAL M. HASSIM, ET AL.,

DAY 28 – MORNING SESSION

(Jury present)
CONNER SKILLING, resumed
CROSS-EXAMINATION (continued)

MR. BRAND

When we concluded cross-examination at the end of the day yesterday I was asking you about the various ways an informant goes about investigating criminal activity for the federal government. Do you remember that?

CONNER SKILLING

Yes.

MR. BRAND

And as we have it from your testimony and the testimony of Agent Farrow, cooperating witnesses typically investigate criminal activity through the use of consensual recordings. And when we say consensual recordings what we're referring to is a recording between an informant and another person with the consent of the informant, isn't that right?

CONNER SKILLING

My consent makes the recording legal.

MR. BRAND

The personal consent of someone like you, Mr. Skilling, who has admitted here in this courtroom to being a con man his entire life — your own personal consent and a hidden micro cassette is enough to begin a federal investigation of private individuals who have never, previous to an encounter with you, been identified as having engaged in criminal conduct. Isn't that true?

CONNER SKILLING

I've been authorized to stop crime before it happens.

MR. BRAND

By encouraging unsuspecting citizens to listen to you by "waving the big pork chop" and "dangling the rib roast," isn't that how you put it?

CONNER SKILLING

I was authorized by Agent Farrow and Mr. Fitzpatrick to make up stories about investment opportunities and possible investors in order to play my role as a corrupt investment banker, to maintain credibility.

MR. BRAND

Why make up stories when you were maintaining that role in real time, with real life stock fraud run through corrupt brokerage firms like Myers Shellac and Solomon Blarney, that you secretly owned?

CONNER SKILLING

That's what you say, Mr. Brand.

MR. BRAND

That's what the U.S. Attorney's office from Eastern District of New York said in an subpoena, issued in June 2006, while you were busy taping my client for the U.S. Attorney's office here in the Southern District — which was a real problem for you, wasn't it, Mr. Skilling?

CONNER SKILLING

No.

MR. BRAND

Mr. Skilling, your cooperation agreement is not with the government in general, across the country. You knew that the fact you made a deal to cooperate with the Southern District of New York didn't mean you couldn't be investigated or prosecuted for crimes by Demetrius Smith, the U.S. Attorney in the Eastern District, who targeted you as a prime suspect in a stock fraud scheme that cost investors over one hundred million dollars in losses — which ultimately resulted in the indictment of over twenty-five stockbrokers. Isn't that true?

CONNER SKILLING

I don't know anything about that.

MR. BRAND

But you do know that after you had your lawyer write a letter to Patrick Fitzpatrick's office about that grand jury subpoena, you never heard from the Eastern District again.

CONNER SKILLING

In substance, no. I never heard from Eastern District after the attorneys and prosecutors dealt together on the Smith matter.

MR. BRAND

They got together and it went away. Fair statement?

CONNER SKILLING

I know they chatted.

MR. BRAND

You chat quite a bit with Mr. Fitzpatrick and Mr. Varlet, don't you? In fact, you chatted with them before taking the stand again today about how to better comport yourself while you testify, isn't that right?

CONNER SKILLING

No. I haven't spoken to them since I began my testimony. Talking to them while I'm on the stand is against the law.

MR. BRAND

When Agent Farrow testified earlier in this proceeding, he stated that he had never done anything to determine the amount of money you made during the ten years he worked as your supervising agent, even though it was his duty to make sure you didn't profit from illegal activity. I'm sure the government attorneys told you about that part of his testimony, before you took the stand. Before it was illegal for you to talk to them.

CONNER SKILLING

I don't recall.

MR. BRAND

Do you recall them asking you about the fraudulent manipulation of a stock called Merrico?

CONNER SKILLING

Don't know.

MR. BRAND

Do you remember hearing about Agent Farrow's testimony, when I asked him in this courtroom, when I asked him, "Even though you chose not to ask, don't you think Conner Skilling should have told you how he amassed the millions of dollars he made while he worked for the FBI?" Did the government lawyers discuss his answer to that question with you?

CONNER SKILLING

I don't remember any discussion like that.

MR. BRAND

Let me read you his answer then. Agent Farrow said this, and these are his words. He said, "I'm certain if I had asked Mr. Skilling how he made this money he would have told me."

Mr. Skilling, now that the defense has subpoenaed your trading records and given them to the government, so that they can finally examine some of the illegal activity you've been engaged in while you worked for them all these years, I would assume Mr. Fitzpatrick and Mr. Varlet have asked you if there are any other trading activities you've engaged in not found in these documents, that they should be concerned about. Would that be correct?

CONNER SKILLING

Yes.

MR. BRAND

And what did you tell them?

CONNER SKILLING

That there was nothing else I could think of.

MR. BRAND

So we can assume, then, that you told them about the brokerage house you opened to pump the Merrico stock, after the Eastern District shut down Myers Shellac and Solomon Blarney. You told them about that, right?

CONNER SKILLING

Mr. Fitzpatrick —

MR. BRAND

I'm Donald Brand. And my question to you is this: When the prosecutors sitting here in this courtroom asked you if there were any other illegal activities you engaged in while working for the Justice Department, defending freedom, did you tell them about Liberty Trust?

CONNER SKILLING

No, for a certain reason.

MR. BRAND

Could that certain reason have something to do with the fact that an assistant district attorney from the Manhattan DA's office, another office you have no cooperation agreement with, is investigating your connection to the Liberty Trust stock firm?

CONNER SKILLING

I — I. I'm not sure.

MR. BRAND

Mr. Skilling, have you received a target letter from the Manhattan DA's office during the course of this proceeding, advising you that you are the subject of a criminal investigation related to the illegal sale and manipulation of publicly traded securities through a brokerage house called Liberty Trust, located at 3240 Commercial Drive, Islip, New York? Yes or no, Mr. Skilling. Yes or no?

CONNER SKILLING

In substance.

Side B
9/18/08

I've been tellin' Fitzie all day, "You got to calm down and stop cryin' like a cunt."

Not to throw a rose, but you took it like a man, like you understand what I always say, "You're bound to run into a couple of potholes no matter how careful you drive."

Insofar as this particular issue, considering the panoply of events, I have an idea on the table to discuss, which I think is better brought out in a private discussion between you and me, face to face, no disrespect to Fitzie.

That's why I said, "Tell Vartie he's got have a discreet conversation with me on this one, 'cause I have great experience with hiccups, which is why I'm very adept at coming up with prospective proposals to ameliorate speed bumps and blips."

So before you give me the speech about how I embarrassed you and how I should have told you in advance about Liberty Trust so you could have just dumped it into the laundry list of connivery Fitzie recited for the jury in his opening statement that they've already forgotten by now because it was two months ago and most of them ain't smart enough to spell CAT. Before you tell me about that, and how even the most inattentive jurors, like that homegirl who's always fallin' asleep 'cause her baby keeps her up all night, how ones like her and that old, toothless orderly whose eyes are always rollin' up in the back of his head, how even they're gonna remember that Brandy had me on the ropes today and that it made us all look bad for no reason. Before you go there let me assure you that I have a very clever plan for maneuvering that lightens the load and gives us a little extra thing to spin around in addition to that.

See, there's a situation afoot that could derail our cart quicker than me getting caught by the shorthairs a couple of times. And it's a little touchy, 'cause the particular situation I'm lookin' at is kinda awkward, which is why I wanted to discuss it on a private basis so that we could use our collective cleverness to create the right kind of groundwork.

And you ain't seen this, no disrespect to you, 'cause you're always facin' toward the bench, when NAACP — that's what I call Hassie's father — shuffles in lookin' upright and decent the way those old time niggers sometimes do, with his gook wife wearin' that same housedress everyday.

And they sit in full view of the jury box with that cute little half-breed, twistin' and huggin' and throwin' kisses whenever Hassie gets a chance to turn around.

Yesterday —

I don't know if you heard it.

She called him.

She shouted, "Daddy!" while the marshals were cuffin' the manacles to Hassie's waist when they was preparing to bring him back to the holding cell, for the midday break.

Well, I'll tell you what, you may have not noticed, but I know the jurors did.

And they saw that glance he threw her, that could've come right out of a made for TV movie.

You know, one of those, "Even though I've been wronged and you've been made to suffer, we're gonna find a way to come out on the other side of this mess, yet" looks.

And I was watchin' this and sayin' to myself, Fitzie is goin' postal 'cause I had a few forgotten details, while the real issue is squirmin' its anklets and pigtails right behind his back, and causin' all kinds of harm.

And then I'm thinkin', "What's gonna happen when the kid sees the video?"

I'm sorry — it don't matter how hardhearted and how much you get them to hate, there ain't gonna be a dry eye in the courtroom when that kid sees her mother for the first time in years, chained to the floor with an arsenal of guns in her face.

And I'll tell you what, whoever did that production should've made her to stop from doin' that dazed and flinchy thing.

Listen, I understand you got good justification for extraordinary measures.

It ain't easy to force a dedicated terrorist to fess up and admit.

But make her look straight into the camera and say it like she means it, for chrissake — not whisper in a monotone — like she's some stubborn little filly finally cowered by the whip.

Don't get me wrong, I saw the craft and the handiwork. Especially when your guys got her to say it's possible botulism could have been in the Dannon the FBI found in her fridge. And that part where she says she's aware that yogurt is commonly served in cafeterias across the country, to millions of American kids.

When I saw that, I says to Lossman, "It's a beaut."

'Cause now you get to tie in to Malik in a way that's plausibly convincing.

Like, why would she say that, if he wasn't telling the truth?

And I says that to Fitzie, I says, "Listen, we're both salesmen. We know exactly what the public wants."

So if we know they want steak, we're not bringin' them a plate of liver.

And let's face it, after they see Hassie's wife up there sayin' she kept extra antibiotics around in case she picked up one of her own infections, the jury's gonna want to stand up and deliver. I don't care what they say about it being common practice amongst scientists of her ilk.

Anyways, no one's gonna remember that after they see her admitting that the projected production numbers for common carp really meant how many would get killed.

Especially after they watch that part where she says she bought Hassie them boxers with pictures of bacterias on the butt from the gift shop at the CDC.

That'll get 'em riled, and fits in with the theory that she looked on poisoning our milk supply as diabolical joke very nicely.

Now alls you need is an officer from the 89th to testify if she potentially wanted to plant Air Force One with poison M&Ms that she could have found a way to do it through a possible connection Hassie likely knew.

You've got that set up already?

I'd say you've got this all buttoned up then.

Which brings me back to the earlier point I was tryin' to make, that you can't let Hassie's kid go cryin' "Mommy" all over your marketing plan, 'cause that could pull all kinds of unnecessary heartstrings and seriously get in the way.

Wait a minute —

I had no idea there was a question as to whether the tape will get used.

Listen, I agree.

It don't give a good impression, having some shivering ninety-pound woman sign a confession when it looks like she's only half-alive.

Not for nothin', but she sorta reminds me of Chief Tanna after he's seen a volcano, which ain't a pretty sight.

So you'll read it into evidence for flavoring.

Okay, I got ya.

Then you'll announce a few weeks later, like an aside, "We regret to inform the court that the prosecution will have to withdraw certain charges in the indictment due to recent information that the video of Mrs. Hassim making her confession has been accidentally lost.

Or inadvertently destroyed —

According to top officials with the FBI."

All right, so now I understand your strategy.

But that still don't change my opinion on Hassie's kid and parents, and the negative effect they could have for you.

Listen, I know we can't have the old man barred 'cause he looks like he could have marched Selma, or a seven-year-old ejected on account of bein' too cute. So I came up with some pre-advice for a plan that's dressed nicely, with a real basis for reality that can be accomplished with just a modicum of effort.

But I sorta need a blessing and an entry point, before I pop this thing —

Which I figure should be when Brandy starts needlin' me about why I told the FBI Merrico was kosher, and how come we edited all my little sideline chats with Rodney out of the mix.

I figure when he asks me about that...and why that last tape broke where it did... that's when I'll pull my Hale Marino.

It's money in the bank.

Take my word on this.

IN THE MATTER OF:
THE UNITED STATES OF AMERICA v.
JAMAL HASSIM ET AL.,

DAY 29- AFTERNOON SESSION

(Trial resumed)
(Jury not present)

THE COURT

I haven't called the jury back from their break because the government has brought a disturbing issue to my attention that needs to be
addressed before trial proceedings can resume. Mr. Fitzpatrick, why
don't you tell the defense lawyers what you told me at the end of Mr.
Skilling's testimony this morning?

MR. FITZPATRICK

Do you want me to do it now? If we could do it with the witness in
the robing room, I think that would probably be best, because I
wanted you to hear from the witness what happened.

THE COURT

Why don't you give the defense an idea of what's going on before
we hear from Mr. Skilling?

MR. FITZPATRICK

I agree judge, other counsel ought to know what's happening here.
It's fine if they all know. It's just that relatives of a defendant who
were seated in the gallery this morning were mouthing things to Mr.
Skilling, those relatives being the parents of Jamal Hassim, and I
wanted the judge to know, because we want to lay the foundation for
expulsion and possible criminal charges for intimidation of a federal
witness. We just wanted to take a few minutes so that the judge can
hear from Mr. Skilling in the robing room rather than open court.

MR. BRAND

The Hassims were mouthing something to Mr. Skilling in the courtroom?

MR. FITZPATRICK

Yes, while we were at the sidebar. I immediately brought it to the attention of Agent Lossman.

THE COURT

Obviously we are going to listen to these charges before Mr. Skilling
returns to continue his testimony today.

MR. BRAND

I have a particular concern about these proceedings because of the
impact they might have on my client, and his family, who do not
have counsel present.

THE COURT

Because of the gravity of these charges, I will hear from the government and Mr. Skilling now. We need to address this issue before
cross-examination continues.

Side A
9/19/08

Admit it. I'm a genius! Let's see if 20/20 gives another look at
their story about Hassie bein' the Big Brother, helping the home-
less, raising himself up from the ghetto, do-gooder son, enlistin' to
fly with the reserves to defend the homeland after his regular tour
was done.

Let them try and retail that now that they got an accusation
against them too.

And it was like I says to Vartie, with regard to this particular
issue, you don't even have to directly participate to have your interests put forward, 'cause I can set all the groundwork. You just come

in on the legal basis to justify it and give it credibility.

I'm the perfect front man for you.

It's like I always say in business, "You need to have a couple of go-to guys to get things kicked off if you want to get a project movin' in the right direction." So you call in one or two to do you a favor. And you go and you piss in their ear, "Hey, do us a favor, take down some of this paper, and put us on the street a little bit."

So we blow a little smoke, and presto!

The whole market's changed.

Now they're sayin', "I don't know about those Hassims. When they had their interview with Katie Couric they sounded so sincere, flashin' pictures of Hassie and his wife, talking through their tears. And it was genuinely heartbreaking, like when the old man said, 'The last time my grandbaby saw her mother, armed commandos in ski masks were draggin' her into a Humvee with a sandbag over her head.' "

So it's good we pulled the trigger, under the tried-and-true theory of "where there's smoke there's fire."

As I'm so fond of sayin', "It don't matter if it comes from grease, kids playin' with matches, or somethin' an arsonist set. Once the public sniffs it, they never lose the scent."

So now that we've got Mom and Pops out of the picture and on the defensive, havin' to say, "We didn't threaten to kill the witness against our son," all them stories they were tellin' about how I'm a crook and you're a bunch of ambitious headline junkies are as good as done.

Before they can say that again, they'll have to explain why Judge Mulligan ejected them from the courtroom for intimidation and the Justice Department is mullin' on what charges to make.

Let them try to talk about how innocent they are now, with the IRS is lookin' into their filings for the last ten years, under allegations their cleaning business was laundering more than just suits.

Now that we have that goin' it won't look so bad when Brandy forces me to admit I purposely put all my assets in Candy's accounts 'cause I don't want nothin' in my name, or that I embellished customers' financial statements to acquire credit for cars.

Look at it this way — now we got a little more latitude when he brings up the child support issue.

And the accusation I hit the first wife.

Which, of course, I would never do — even though she deserved it.

But he'll bring that up. You're right.

Yeah, and the Mitchell Kinsley incident.

Now, wait a minute —

That was Candy's fault too.

I would have never had to punch him if she hadn't told me he was flirting.

Which, by the way, is what he had coming.

I don't care if he's in a wheelchair because of MS.

It's what any man would do.

But hey, at least now when Brandy brings that up, and how I sold all the Porsches off my lot before the bank foreclosed, even though they were collateral, you're all set up to confidently say, "When a citizen's risking his life to protect the public from terrorist leaders and their criminal families — a few minor indiscretions shouldn't get in the way."

I don't know, but if I were you, I'd be sayin' "We fuckin'

stepped in it when we signed on the dotted line with Conner, 'cause he hits more home runs than Sammy Sosa."

I was sayin' that to Vartie yesterday, I was sayin, "I start everything and leave."

Instigation and leaving.

Alls you need to do is pick the carcass after I'm through, sippin' champagne in first class on the way back home.

And while I'm doin' that, you just move in and finish 'em, like a relief pitcher in the ninth. Like you did with Hale Marino, after he came in to watch me when we were doing that stockbroker from Fargo.

Remember that schlemiel?

Sittin' there in the gallery all tan and confident, like he don't have a care in the world, 'cause his trial is three months away, and he's in that delusional stage when they still think they can win — even though the chance of that happening ain't no better than the chance Bank of America had of gettin' their loan monies on my leasing company paid, when I told 'em, "Stand in line behind the student loan department from the State of New Jersey, and the El San Juan Casino and Chelsea National Bank, my former landlord at the Park Towers — and the fuckin' cable guy.

Take a ticket and get ready to wait until you have to write it off."

But Halie was a stubborn son of a bitch.

He just couldn't get it through his head that he could get convicted when he hadn't done nothin' but run his mouth, even though you told him.

And I remember this Fitzie —

When you told him and his lawyer that they had to take this seriously, 'cause half the people in jail today are in on a conspiracy ticket.

He just couldn't come around to the concept that if you say something stupid, even if you didn't mean it, and didn't do nothin' to follow it up, that we can use it to put you behind bars on a theory of what you were thinking. Like it's un-American or something that some jailhouse snitch or some cute little guy like myself can ruin your life by putting the finger on you and sayin' you're guilty so he can make his sentence a little lighter in the loafers.

He actually believed he could take me on, and beat the rap.
What a moron!
I remember thinkin' that when I seen him smilin' his caps at me there in the courtroom.
And this is after I already had him on tape sayin' he wanted to kill me for chiselin' him out of stock on that Australian insurance deal, where Rod sold the shares from his father's insurance company to HIG.
And Halie had a problem with that, sayin' I schmuck-baited him out of cheap Flitch stock in his account so I could stockpile it in my own for the run-up when the merger was announced...which of course, I would never do.
But he got himself all lathered up anyways, saying he was gonna put a bullet through my head and cut my tongue out and all that other gobbledygook when I took him to Sparks Steakhouse to explain my side of the situation, after we had a few glasses of wine and started talkin' about how the wise guys do it when they have a beef.

And it was perfect, 'cause we got him on conspiracy to commit murder.
That was the best!

And then the fruitcake shows up at the stockbroker's trial, to get a free look. Like he's comin' in to test-drive a car.

That's when I says to Farrow, "No way. Like, I ain't gonna sit up here and sweat bullets on the witness stand while some dude with a gripe is givin' me dirty looks and shoppin' my testimony."

And Farrow says, " The courtroom gallery is open to the public. The only way to get rid of someone is if they're openly disruptive.

Or if they do somethin' that makes you fear for your life."

Luckily, I've always been a fast learner, as exemplified by the way I slipped past Brandy when he asked about the break on that last tape I made of Hassie, when I says, "What we have here are arbitrary breakdowns. Simply flipping a tape, or starting a new tape can cause this...so the breakdowns tape-by-tape are utterly arbitrary being that conversations start and stop without any attention paid to where the tapes start and stop."

I thought that was a pretty clever answer that didn't raise too many eyebrows, if I don't say so myself.

And I'll tell you what, juror number six agreed.

I could tell 'cause she was nodding when I was sayin' that.

So I know I got her vote.

And it couldn't be better, 'cause Brandy was totally off his game.

Which is what I figured would happen after the marshals escorted Hassie's family out of the courthouse at the conclusion of our back-room chat.

I just wish we could've thrown that old spook down for ten years like we did with Marino.

I know.

You don't have to remind me.

Halie got slammed because he was already a named defendant in an ongoing case, whereas old man Hassim isn't —
Yet.

I prefer instant gratification, personally speaking.
But you're right.

There's always time for that.

BREAKING NEWS:
COLLAPSE OF INSURANCE GIANT ROCKS AUSTRALIAN ECONOMY

Australia's Second Largest Insurer Insolvent,
Amid Charges of Accounting Fraud

SYDNEY, Australia, September 29 — Australia has experienced a shocking number of corporate collapses this year, and it has not gone unnoticed by authorities that two of the highest profile disasters have something in common. The connection is Rodney Flitch, an insurance executive-turned-venture capitalist, who resigned from his role as director of HIG Insurance Ltd late yesterday, amid accusations by regulators that he failed to disclose the full details of reinsurance contracts to auditors assessing the valuation of Flitch International Insurance (FII), before he sold Flitch to HIG. According to authorities familiar with the case, unreported reserve shortfalls at Flitch International, variously estimated between sixty and two hundred and fifty million dollars, had a drastic effect on earnings reports for the financial year ending in June 2003, allowing

Flitch to declare a pre-tax profit of $8.6 million instead of a $21.9 million dollar loss. Based on this inflated accounting, and a sudden run-up of Flitch International stock stateside, underwritten by Myers Shellac and Solomon Blarney, two brokerage houses in New York currently under criminal indictment for securities fraud, HIG acquired Flitch for three hundred million in September 2003. These questionable transactions, which ended up losing HIG an estimated six hundred million dollars within a year of the Flitch takeover, had a devastating effect on HIG's solvency, and are blamed for its ultimate failure.

Mr. Flitch, who was photographed sipping margaritas poolside at one of Melbourne's choicest hotels, showed no sign of concern as his lawyers were pleading with a Sydney court not to freeze his assets in connection with the HIG collapse, and the collapse of Tel One Ltd, a telecommunications company he ran that was placed into liquidation last March with up to two billion dollars in debt under circumstances disturbingly similar to those that brought about the demise of HIG. In a statement released early today, Mr. Flitch stated that he was "shocked at the extent of the losses" from both companies, and is "sorry about the terrible fate that has befallen those involved with HIG," most of whom where union members and small policyholders in Australia and the United States.

Due to an uncanny prescience that many authorities view with suspicion, Mr. Flitch has little concern about sharing the financial devastation experienced by his customers and stockholders. He sold all his shares in HIG and Tel One in the months before each company collapsed. His attorneys maintain these sales were perfectly legal. Both stocks are now nearly worthless.

Side A
9/29/08

What are you gonna do now?

I don't see as you got any choice.

You're gonna continue to cross-examine Colonel May like noth-in' happened, 'cause nothin' did.

Vartie told me you had him backed into a corner yesterday with questions about overstaying a furlough when he served in Vietnam.

Too bad it worked out that it happened 'cause his mother died.

But those are the chances you take when you have to dig that deep into the past.

All in all, I hear it's goin' well, especially when you started hittin' him with those questions like, "Did you know Jamal Hassim said that, 'It's the Muslim duty to defend Muslim interests against the Great Satan by all means possible?' "

I don't care how good he is, no one is solid enough to head that one off.

So don't give me all this crybaby shit about how we're gonna lose this trial 'cause of Rodney, and that it don't look good that my brokers helped him promote his stock, which we shouldn't have been doin' by means of my cooperation with you.

None of that is gonna matter, and you know why?

'Cause people generally don't give a shit how many scumbag moves you pull on other people, as long as you don't pull those moves on them.

Let's face it, most of our jurors can't barely scrape up enough jack to buy themselves a hot dog from the lunch wagon. Which is why none of them is gonna be gettin' all hot under the collar about a bunch of rich investors who lost money on stocks they never heard of. Especially since those people never give them enough respect when they cash them out at K-Mart or serve them their steak dinners anyways.

So for them, Rodney Flitch ain't a problem.

He's like them poor bastards getting slaughtered in Baghdad, a hundred at a time.

He don't matter.

He's just a concept.

He don't personally affect their lives.

Okay, so juror number eleven might take issue with that theory 'cause she's a member of the Confectioner's Union, and they had a health insurance policy with HIG which ain't worth the paper it's written on anymore.

Look, it's a problem, I won't deny it, but it could be much worse.

I mean, it ain't like we emptied her out of her life savings or nothin'.

Besides, I've made some significant eye contact with her.

Never underestimate the power of makin' some three hundred pound pachyderm who ain't been laid in sixteen years feel like you can see past her gut and the stubble on her chin into her innermost Marilyn Monroe.

Hey, you might not like my style, but I can assure you that Rod charmed the pants off of her and all the other ladies when he was in, 'cause he's a debonair kinda guy.

You're right.

Brandy's gonna make a big deal about it, and try to tie it into an argument that I only get the innocent indicted so I can keep the real bad guys for myself.

I can just hear him now, sayin' that the only deals I investigate are ones I can't personally put into play and put a chop on.

He's gonna do that for sure.

But you got Malik, you got the videos from Al-Jazeera, you got human remains bein' sent home by the military every day —

Plus you got the Attorney General stumpin' on how Hassie's sleeper cell was the biggest domestic terror organization to ever threaten the interest of public security and the safety of the United States.

Last time I looked, that still makes you the odds on favorite, and Hassie the horse that got stuck in the gate.

So you'll just stay the course for now, and continue your line of attack.

Hey, and from what I can see, it wouldn't hurt to suggest that Colonel May has a little bit of guilt in this too.

I'd say he's got more on the line than his own reputation, for allowing a known terrorist sympathizer to work on his staff.

Was it due to incompetence or complicity?

That's what I would ask.

Well, I don't know what you mean by that.

I think I'm as qualified as anyone here to analyze the situation.

What am I missing?

Okay, so we have three questionable witnesses.

So what?

We've overcome that dozens of times.

But never in a case where the whole world is watching, where a major piece of evidence is about to hit the cutting room floor...

Well, that could be a problem.

I'll admit that to you.
But I know the animals I'm dealing with here.

They won't allow us to lose.

IN THE MATTER OF:

UNITED STATES OF AMERICA v.
JAMAL M. HASSIM, ET AL.,

DAY 36 - MORNING SESSION

(At the sidebar)
(Jury not present)

THE COURT
We have a number of issues to address this morning before we bring the jury in. First, there is a renewed request by defense council to cross-examine Ahn Hassim. Does the government have a response?

MR. FITZPATRICK
Your Honor, the government cannot make Ahn Hassim available to the defense for this purpose. She is a high-value detainee, whose whereabouts must be kept secret as a matter of national security. Agent Lossman, who was present throughout her interrogation, has been made available to defense counsel for impeachment purposes, but that's as far as the Justice Department will allow us to go.

THE COURT

Certainly an examination of Agent Lossman will give the defense some insight into the circumstances of Mrs. Hassim's confession.

MR. BRAND

Ahn Hassim's written confession was read into the record based on representations by the government that a verbal confession, recorded at the time the written one was signed, would also be made available. It was this representation that the court relied upon when it allowed the written confession into evidence. Your Honor asked the government during colloquy on this issue how the court could be sure Ahn Hassim's confession wasn't a result of coercive treatment. At that time, the government assured the court that their tape would demonstrate that she had not been subjected to aggressive interrogation techniques. As you recall, we objected to the argument that such a recording would provide conclusive evidence as to how this confession was come by, and your Honor reserved a final ruling on the issue until after the tape was played. Now after weeks of delay, we're told there is no tape, so what we're left with is a written document signed under unknown circumstances by an unindicted co-conspirator detained at an undisclosed location, that we are now being told is unavailable for any kind of questioning. This is fundamentally unfair and in flagrant violation of a defendant's right to confront an accuser.

THE COURT

The defense brings up valid concerns. How does the government respond?

MR. FITZPATRICK

Your Honor, Special Agent Lossman is a fourteen-year veteran with the FBI. He testified fully — or virtually fully — that no excessive force occurred. But if Mr. Brand would like to question him again on this issue, we have no objection.

MR. BRAND
Mr. Lossman is an agent of the government, and can hardly be relied upon to provide testimony that will be helpful to the defense. Why can't the government make Mrs. Hassim available through a live satellite video feed from wherever she is so that she can be questioned in real time while remaining in custody? That way the right to confrontation can be satisfied, and her location can remain undisclosed. This is not a perfect solution, but it is a compromise the defense is willing to make due to the circumstances of her detention.

MR. FITZGERALD
The kind of exchange Mr. Brand suggests is not possible since it would involve discussion of classified activities. It is out of the question.

MR. BRAND
As a matter of law a defendant should be allowed to question his accusers. The government's position on this issue forces us to fight at shadows that can't be grabbed at or confronted.

THE COURT
I'm inclined to agree with Mr. Brand. The defense has a right, under the confrontation clause, to question this witness.

MR. FITZPATRICK
It is the government's position that Mr. Hassim is essentially stateless, owing to his stated allegiance to the extremist cause of transna-

tional terrorism, and therefore not entitled to customary protections under Federal law.

MR. BRAND

Jamal Hassim is a citizen of the United States, being tried in a Federal courthouse, which entitles him to be treated like any other Federal suspect.

MR. FITZPATRICK

When we're dealing with captured individuals who we know or believe to be terrorists the debate over rights cannot be confined to arguments that are strictly legal. We should also ask if we are doing everything we can to protect innocent lives. That is the most important question to ask.

MR. BRAND

Whose innocent lives are we talking about here? Jamal Hassim is innocent until proven guilty, and Ahn Hassim has never been formally charged.

MR. FITZPATRICK

It is our duty to bring terrorists to justice whenever possible in the interest of protecting the people. We respectfully ask your Honor for flexibility on this issue, and wish to remind the court that U.S. policy prohibits U.S. personnel from engaging in cruel, inhumane, and degrading treatment of prisoners inside and outside American borders.

MR. BRAND

We have never been given any proof or assurance that Mrs. Hassim was interrogated by agents from the U.S. government. She could have been interrogated by operatives in the Philippines, who have a long history of using torture, or law enforcement agencies from other countries operating as third or fourth parties to the process that might have human rights records that are even worse. We just have no idea, which makes an in-depth discovery on this subject vital.

MR. FITZPATRICK

There are cases when a local government may want to prosecute a subject or choose to cooperate in the transfer of a suspect to a third country. I'm not saying which of these alternatives is the case with Mrs. Hassim, but what I can say is that interrogations of Al Qaeda and Taliban suspects overseas have produced information that have helped save American lives.

THE COURT

Mr. Fitzpatrick, you understood when you read Mrs. Hassim's confession into the record that it would open up the door for a request of cross-examination, which, unless you can provide me with more compelling arguments, I am close to ordering.

MR. FITZPATRICK

Your Honor, I would like the opportunity to confer with my department head about our position on this.

Side B
9/30/08

I'll tell you the same thing I said to Vartie when he broke the news to me, I said, "When was it Mulligan grew a set of balls?"

I mean, not for nothin' but he's a little old, ain't he?

I still say the drama made him do it, with Sheik Youssof screamin', "torturers!" when you got to that part about third party interrogations. So Mulligan probably felt he had no choice in the face of that. Which made him feel like he had to say, "Both sides need to brief me on the issues."

In my opinion it's just a delay tactic to give the appearance he's bein' fair to both sides, before he rules to let the show go on — like he did when he caught us inflating how many investors lost money in the Suarez trial.

You know, when he called your misstatement on the numbers, "Overly zealous repartee."

How did he put it?

Due to, "prosecutorial exuberance." That was great!

As I've always been known to say, "If you gotta pull moves, it's better in front of a Reagan appointee, 'cause you know he's inclined go our way."

Which, if he follows your suggestion and strikes the confession from the record, will be the most plausible thing for him to do.

He can just say to the jurors, "Pretend you didn't hear it when you go back to the jury room and deliberate, and don't consider it when you get together and make up your minds. You are not to speculate about the reasons why this evidence is no longer part of this trial, and its absence should not affect or influence your verdict in this case."

Even though we all know it's a little bit of a smokescreen, judges do that every day.

That's my Jimmy-the-Greek wager on what's gonna happen.

But if it don't, you know where to find me.

The scenery ain't too exciting, but at least it's tax-free.

Wait.

So what you're saying is, you're not gonna take a chance on which way he's gonna decide?

Meaning what?

You think this situation is so far out of control, that Mulligan might not place his bet with the house this particular time?

So you're going to revise certain positions.

Hey listen, we're traders, so we know how to adapt in a pinch.

It's called elephants through a revolving door.

Meaning I, okay, notwithstanding the tremendous commonality between us, understand about dealing out of declining markets from the equity side. So I guess what I'm asking is the operational approach for doing that when you're using the law.

I'll have to wait to find that out until tomorrow, when you publicly announce?

Hey come on, we've been friendly, relationship-wise, exceeding probably, on balance, ten years. Can't you give me a little teaser? I'm just lookin' for a pre-sniff of the aroma. I don't need the whole roast.

All right. All right.

We'll cover it in ultra-detail sometime later in a private conversation.

Hey listen, you're talking to me. I know all about stuff bein' too sensitive to discuss over the phone.

THE WHITE HOUSE
WASHINGTON

TO THE SECRETARY OF DEFENSE AND THE ATTORNEY GENERAL

In accordance with the Constitution and consistent with the laws of the United States, including the Authorization for Use of Military Force Joint Resolution (Public Law 107-40):

The President of the United States and Commander in Chief of the U.S. armed forces has hereby DETERMINED for the United States of America that:

(1) Jamal M. Hassim, who is under the control of the Department of Justice, is, and at the time he was arrested on June 21, 2006, an enemy combatant;

(2) Mr. Hassim is closely associated with Al Qaeda, an international terrorist organization with which the United States is at war;

(3) Mr. Hassim engaged in conduct that constituted hostile and war-like acts, including conduct in preparation for acts of international terrorism that had the aim to cause injury to or adverse effects on the United States;

(4) Mr. Hassim possesses intelligence, including intelligence about personnel and activities of Al Qaeda that if communicated to the U.S., would aid U.S. efforts to prevent attacks by Al Qaeda on the United States or its armed forces, other government personnel, or citizens;

(5) Mr. Hassim represents a continuing, present, and

grave danger to the national security of the United States, and detention of Mr. Hassim is necessary to prevent him from aiding Al Qaeda in its efforts to attack the United States or its armed forces, other government personnel, or citizens;

(6) It is in the interest of the United States, and consistent with U.S. law and the laws of war that the Secretary of Defense detain Mr. Hassim as an enemy combatant.

Accordingly, the Attorney General is directed to surrender Mr. Hassim to the Secretary of Defense, and the Secretary of Defense is directed to receive Mr. Hassim from the Department of Justice and to detain him as an enemy combatant.

IN THE MATTER OF:

UNITED STATES OF AMERICA v. AMAL M. HASSIM, ET AL.,

DAY 37 - MORNING SESSION
8:30 am

(Jury not present)

THE COURT

Early this morning, the government petitioned this court to dismiss the indictment against Mr. Hassim without prejudice, based on a declaration, signed by the President of the United States, that re-designates Mr. Hassim's status. As I stated to Mr. Fitzpatrick when he met with me in chambers, before I make a ruling on this motion, I'd like to hear from the defense.

MR. BRAND

Your Honor, this action the government has taken is outrageous! The defense requests that your Honor issue an emergency order to block Mr. Hassim's transfer out of this jurisdiction until we have a chance to meet with him, and formally object to this unprecedented act of judicial manipulation.

MR. FITZPATRICK

Your Honor, the FBI has recently obtained secret information implicating Jamal Hassim in an ongoing terrorist threat. His status has been re-designated in order to thwart him from further plotting against U.S. interests in this country and overseas.

MR. BRAND

Judge, this is a blatant and desperate attempt on the part of the prosecution to evade civilian trial guarantees. We will move to continue this trial, unless the government intends to drop all pending criminal charges against Mr. Hassim with prejudice.

MR. FITZPATRICK

Your Honor, the government shouldn't be penalized because of a preventative action it was forced to take in the name of national security.

MR. BRAND

Judge, this court should not allow the government to try my client on similar charges in two different venues, with drastically different evidentiary standards and procedural rules. Mr. Hassim is an American citizen. This court has a duty to defend his constitutional rights.

THE COURT

Is Mr. Hassim a federal defendant, or is he a terrorism suspect? It seems to me unfair for the government to disrupt this trial so it can try Mr. Hassim as an unlawful combatant in front of a military tribunal, and at the same time expect this court to allow it to reserve the right to come back and try him again on federal charges in a case it has chosen to interrupt.

MR. FITZPATRICK

Let me just say, your Honor, that we are as surprised as anyone about this dramatic turn of events. We were just advised about this a few hours ago, and respectfully request that your Honor give us the opportunity to confer with the Attorney General before we submit a final argument on this issue.

THE COURT

I expect to be briefed by both sides no later than tomorrow. Be advised that I'm signing an order that Mr. Hassim should not be moved until then.

MR. FITZPATRICK

With all due respect, your Honor does not have that power, now that custody of Mr. Hassim has been transferred to the Department of Defense.

THE COURT

Mr. Fitzpatrick, until this court rules otherwise, Mr. Hassim is also a federal defendant, and I expect that the government will keep him at the Manhattan Correctional Center until the issue of his legal status is resolved.

BREAKING NEWS
FEDERAL JUDGE REVERSES "DO NOT MOVE HIM" ORDER

Amid Charges of Foul Play on Both Sides, Charges Are Dropped in the Jamal Hassim Case.

NEW YORK, New York, October 2 — After pursuing a conventional criminal case against Jamal Hassim for two years, the government has abruptly changed course, and agreed to dismiss all criminal charges against him with prejudice, which means they cannot be refiled. This decision was reached after William T. Mulligan III, the presiding judge in Mr. Hassim's eight-week trial, indicated he would allow defense lawyers to file papers opposing Mr. Hassim's transfer to Defense Department custody, as long as the criminal case was active.

According to the government, Mr. Hassim's sudden re-designation from criminal defendant to "enemy combatant" was the result of recent intelligence gathered from a high-level Al Qaeda detainee who had heard Major Hassim praising the September 11th terrorist attacks, and identified him as an Al Qaeda "sleeper" operative tasked with executing acts of terrorism on U.S. soil.

The FBI has released information that two other detainees also confirmed that while serving as an Air Force pilot in Afghanistan, Major Hassim visited Al Qaeda training camps where he consorted with suicide bombers, trained insurgents in the use of counter-surveillance techniques, and pledged his service to bin Laden. This, and other classified information "too sensitive" to be released, caused top officials at the Pentagon to conclude that Mr. Hassim was a "flight risk and a danger to the community," making the continuation of a public trial a "major threat" to national security. At the status hearing in front of Judge Mulligan earlier today, Donald Brand, Mr. Hassim's legal council, dismissed these new allegations as "hearsay beaten out of desperate prisoners that wouldn't be admitted under rules of evidence" in a federal court.

Over the course of an unusually contentious proceeding, during which Mr. Brand repeatedly questioned the reliability of the new "evidence" against his client and Judge Mulligan expressed numerous misgivings about the timing of United States attorney's motion to dismiss, government lawyers maintained that the need to protect the public from "the imminent threat" posed by Major Hassim was more important to the "defense of the nation" than the completion of his criminal trial.

Concluding that he lacked the power to compel the government to prosecute Jamal Hassim in his courtroom, Judge Mulligan revoked his emergency order to hold Major Hassim at the Manhattan Correctional Center, and agreed to allow the case against Tarak Youssof, the other defendant in the Hassim trial, to be appended to a pre-existing case against seven parishioners of his mosque, in which he had been listed as an unnamed co-conspirator. Those defendants, who have been held in a federal detention center in Atlanta for nearly two years on charges of conspiracy to provide material support to a terrorist organization, are expected to go on trial next spring.

Side A
10/02/08

Kabaam! Man, you fuckin' nailed 'em!
As I'm so fond of saying, we may have a modest amount of guilt,

but we got no shame! Absolutely none!

I mean, you crafted it so artful, you even made me blush.

Me! Of all people. And you know how hard that is to do. But I'll tell you what, you worked yourself outta your position like George fucking Soros, in that you made the market come to you. It's like I always tell my brokers, "If you run into a quality problem, you gotta be ready to adjust. You gotta cure it or kill it, but whatever you do, don't wait for a natural correction — 'cause that's the way you find yourself under the bus."

I'll tell you the truth, I didn't think you had it in ya.

It just don't come natural to think of a bunch of Poindexters doin' the down and dirty, which from a PR perspective, is a little bit of a plus. Not for nothin', but after all these years of workin' together, even I didn't think pencil necks like you had the stomach to play it that tough.

Hey, not that I blame ya —

If I was in your position, I'd do it like that too.

I mean, why build credibility if you're not gonna use it?

As I've always been known to so brilliantly observe, "What's the point of bulkin' up your muscle, if you're only plannin' on hittin' like a girl?"

And I know you agree with that advice, after what I seen you do.

Still, it's too bad you had to lose out on a conviction.

If I was you, I'd be pissed about that too.

But look at it this way, you bought yourself two years or three years of puttin' Hassie on ice.

Then you'll have one of your colleagues go up in front of another grand jury in Atlanta or Charleston or some other jurisdiction with some slightly different charges, and get another indictment goin' right before Brandy reaches the Supreme Court on the question of Hassie's constitutional rights.

I'm on you with this one. You know what they say about great minds thinking alike. And it's the perfect switch-up.

They'll write him up for receiving military training from Al Qaeda.

Making false statements.

Use of an unconventional weapon.

I got ya.

Okay.

So we're both on the same page on this in sum and substance.

Which means you still come out on this relatively unfettered from a legal point of view.

Hey, as we like to say in business, it's a good leverage play to manage the yield. Meaning, you still got a lock on this one, it'll just take a little longer than we hoped for to close out the deal.

Meanwhile, you shuffled Hassie outta public view in a very creative way.

Look at it like this; you saved a dicey position with a good cross-trade.

And you can't beat the location.

I don't care how much survival training the Air Force put into this guy. There's only so long anyone can last in a windowless cement cell the size of shoebox not knowin' what month it is, or what time — with nothin' to read and no one to talk to — before their brain is fried.

And you're right that the timing is perfect.

I mean, what politician is gonna risk being called soft on terrorism with elections just a few months away? It's like you say, there ain't gonna be no one willing to put their career on the line for his sorry ass.

Our boy's in for the extended stay.

Take it from me, he's gonna crack open like one of my coconuts after a few months livin' twenty-four-seven under fluorescent light, bein' fed through the door, followed by cameras every minute of his life.

As we like to say in Brooklyn, you got a vice grip on his balls.

Which is good insofar as it will further stimulate his thought process and make him more flexible, as we like to so cleverly say.

'Cause Hassie now understands what we understand —

That he's fully boxed in with no chance of escape.

It's like I always told my brokers, "You gotta break 'em down, and get them to see there ain't no cause for hope." After beatin' their head against the wall for enough time, even the most belligerent ones eventually give up the ghost. That is, unless you get unlucky and run into a stubborn case, and they go to the SEC, to which I say "big deal." They ain't got no teeth anyways. Let them file whatever complaint. I just open another office somewhere else, in someone else's name.

I know, I know.

That theory only works if you don't try to bribe a broker wearin' a badge. But look at it this way, if I hadn't made that little mistake, you'd likely still be doin' narcotics in some forgotten courtroom.

Which, thanks to that little problem with my colleague in Australia, you could likely be doin' again?

You're right, that sucks, all joking aside.

But luckily for you, I've developed an ancillary situation as a sort of consolation, which I was gonna keep as a surprise —

That additionally, probably, could be developed very quickly to provide some high-octane gas for the engine — after you address the issue with your boss, and make sure the department is amenable to giving us the liberty to move ahead.

Which is why I said to Mingo the other day, "Pay attention, 'cause I'm the brightest guy you ever knew," while I was down at the ANZ Bank, signin' off on the paperwork to put my licensing through.

And it couldn't be better, 'cause they got the whole thing rigged up with gaming consultants and probity guidance and international companies and all.

So, say a guy in Omaha wants to play a little poker. He just has to log onto my website. Or, if he wants to bet the under/over on the White Sox or the Corn Husters or whatever the case may be — he can dial up my 1-800 number. I got a bunch of youngsters workin' outta my spare bedroom, waiting for his call.

Check it out on your computer.

Sureshotgaming. com

My digital blackjack tables are bein' beamed out right now from an office in downtown Port Vila.

Hey, tell Malikie when you see him at his sentencing next month, the roulette wheel's always on.

And it couldn't be better, 'cause it's all legal here, even if it isn't in Ohio or Australia or anywhere else besides London, that ain't some third-world cash box with a tax-free zone.

Which sets up perfectly, 'cause my agents are a bunch of knockaround guys who used to work the lines at Pinnacle and Bo Dog and all them big international gambling sites in the Dominican Republic and Costa Rica.

So we're dealing with the highest level, and they're all degenerates.

They'll bet on two cockroaches runnin' across the floor.

This is a bunch of swashbuckling Americans with a proclivity for high wire action, lookin' to send some earn home.

So I says to them, "You need to hook me up on a teleconference with management at your former locations, so we can have an informal meeting, and chat globally on how we can repatriate some of these profits back into the States."

And they were all over that like flies on shit.

Zip, zip, zip.

I'll tell ya, it's a perfect foundation that's been laid.

So I've already set up some trans-Pacific conversations with some of these characters so I can capture them over a series of nice, pleasant little meetings — which as you know and I know, won't have to go much past hellos.

I mean, I really don't need to make any new friends, 'cause I'm happy with my old friends — but I figure this could give you a nice little sector rotation with some of them wire and gambling statutes you've been wantin' to pin on these guys.

As you know, and as I'm so fond of saying, "all boats float on a rising tide."

Meaning, if we re-channel the focus, and give them a whiff of something that puts some fresh meat on their plate, your bosses will likely give you a break on the way things went down with the Hassim case.

'Cause this is one of them situations that's like spitting on the floor.

As in, there's no way you can miss.

Trust me when I tell you that they're gonna want this feather for their cap.

Especially after I describe in excruciating detail the extensive conversations where I specifically heard them say they were targeting their websites to underage kids.

And this is groundbreaking, Eliot Spitzer-type stuff, with news conferences, worldwide manhunts and headlines, internationally speaking, that can really put your office on the map.

Think about it — you could bust a billion dollar global business with connections to banks and credit card companies.

No disrespect, but I never met a U.S. attorney yet that ain't temperamentally suitable towards publicity like that.

And what's even better is that by the time we're ready for trial on this, in one year or two years or whatever the case may be, no one but few bleeding hearts will remember who the fuck Hassie is.

Or, that his case had any association with me.

VISIT TO NAVY BRIG

VIDEOTAPE 1

JANUARY 12, 2009

Participants:

JAMAL HASSIM = JAMAL MOHAMMAD HASSIM
BRAND = DONALD BRAND
OFFICER = OFFICER

Abbreviations   (UI) = Unintelligible
                   .... = Incomplete Thought
                   * * * = Redaction

---

* * *

BRAND: [Enters the room with Officer] [To Jamal
                    Hassim] Jamal, it's good to see you.

JAMAL HASSIM: [Trying to stand up] In the Name of God,
                    the merciful, the compassionate, she said
                    you would be here. When I asked, "When
                    comes God's help?" she told me, "Surely
                    God's help is nigh."

BRAND: Jamal, the government has informed me
                    that this interview may be recorded.
                    [Whispering] Guards are only supposed

to give you orders. You know that right?

JAMAL HASSIM: She is not a cow broken to plow the earth or to water the tillage! There is no blemish on her.

BRAND: Okay. Jamal, listen to me. It's taken three months for me to get permission to see you and we only have an hour. There are many things we need to discuss before that lady standing outside the partition comes in and tells me I have to leave, so I need your full attention.

JAMAL HASSIM: Yes, yes. Of course...

BRAND: I have a letter from your father I've been given permission to read.

JAMAL HASSIM: Oh, God, my father. [Rocking] It's been so long.

BRAND: [Looking in his accordion folder] Let me see. Ah, here.

JAMAL HASSIM: [Coughs. Wipes his eyes] Excuse me.

BRAND: [Pulling out the letter] Jamal, are you okay?

JAMAL HASSIM: It's freezing in here. Can you ask them if I can have a sweater, and some socks? It's

	very hard to sleep.
BRAND:	I'll do that.
JAMAL HASSIM:	And a watch. So I know what time to pray.
BRAND:	Is there anything else?
JAMAL HASSIM:	I've made peace with the rest of it. [Coughs]
BRAND:	Okay, let me start reading then, so we don't waste time [Clears throat] In the name of God, the merciful, the compassionate. Dearest Son [Pause] I am forced to communicate with you in this manner because there are no others available to me, now that I find myself under criminal indictment, having to do with the false accusations of that contemptible man. (May God punish him.) I am not writing so that you should worry about that. It is not a burden beyond what I have the strength to bear. I am writing to let you know that we sold the house in Chicago, and have moved in with your uncle Omar. It is easier for us to live a reasonable life this way, since no one knows us here. Also, you should know that your lovely Aseelah and your mother send their love. She is our blessing, your darling child, and she helps to keep us strong. She wants you to know that she goes to the Muslim

Community Center twice a week after class, and that she prays every day for you and for her mother, who we still receive no word on, and about whom we have the greatest fears — especially now, that we have lost all contact with her family. We have no idea what happened, but it is certain they have either been arrested or displaced. Their phone has been disconnected, and a letter we sent two months ago was recently returned in the mail. Your mother is convinced they must have gotten caught up in the winter offensive that the government launched against mountain villages on Mindanao and Jolo island to disrupt what they say are newly identified Al Qaeda networks there —

JAMAL HASSIM: [Shouting] No, no!

DONALD BRAND: Jamal, you've got to get a grip on yourself, or the people here won't let this interview go on.

JAMAL HASSIM: [Breathing heavily] When did it — when did this start?

BRAND: Maybe four or five weeks ago.

JAMAL HASSIM: That's why they re-classified me —

BRAND:	That happened in October. It's January now, Jamal.
JAMAL HASSIM:	She was trying to tell me (UI) but I couldn't understand. She said, "You must fulfill the covenant." May God forgive me, I couldn't tell what she meant. [Pause] How many have died?
BRAND:	I don't know. I don't think any figures have been released. Yesterday I read that members of a secret Special Operations unit were deployed into a number of jungle villages to help the Marines and government troops execute attacks. I know they've been using spy satellites and AC-130 gunships for support...There might have also been some F-15 airstrikes on primary targets...I'm not sure about that, though. [Pause] I know they got some big-time separatist leadership guys. They've been making a big deal over identifying the remains some guy named Abu Chowdry. [Pause] I remember thinking I recognized that name. [Pause] Didn't he work for you?
JAMAL HASSIM:	Now I know why you were screaming! [Pounding table] Forgive me! [Crying] Oh why, why, why?
BRAND:	Jamal, get a hold of yourself. The guard is

looking in.

JAMAL HASSIM: I'm the package leader here. I'll take the missile. I should have done it long ago. I will do it. I will do it for you. I'm ready now. I will do it. I swear to you I will...Oh, Ahn...

BRAND: Jamal, we have to move on to discussing some important issues about your case. I have to be sure that you're with me.

JAMAL HASSIM: I'm with you, Donald. But I have to make sure you're with me.

BRAND: I think I've proven that over the years. [Pause] What are you driving at?

JAMAL HASSIM: I'm guilty.

BRAND: What?

JAMAL HASSIM: I want you to plead me out. I'll agree to anything they want me to stipulate to, as long as they drop the charges against my father, and let Ahn go free.

BRAND: Jamal, I cannot in good conscience...

JAMAL HASSIM: Allow me to save my wife and my father who knew nothing about my terrorist activities? If you don't have the conscience to do that, then don't ever come back here again.

BRAND: Jamal, I'm begging you, don't give up now.
                        The government stopped your trial because
                        they were losing. You understand that, don't
                        you?

JAMAL HASSIM: Of course they are losing. The Lord knows
                        very well those that do corruption.

BRAND: This is not a spiritual debate.

JAMAL HASSIM: You're right. It's not. I'm guilty. I should
                        have listened to her when she begged me to
                        get away, but I was too eager. I wanted to
                        save the business, but she warned me, she
                        said, that man will destroy us. God forgive
                        me, I told her, "Why would anyone want to
                        do that?"

BRAND: That does not make you a terrorist.

JAMAL HASSIM: Yes, I'm afraid it does.

BRAND: Jamal, I want to remind you that it is proba-
                        ble government agents are listening to this
                        conversation.

JAMAL HASSIM: Good. These are my terms. Let my wife go
                        free. Stop persecuting my father, and I will
                        (UI) everything. But first, I must have proof

that the indictment against my father has been dropped, and Ahn has been released.

BRAND: Jamal, Jamal. Your case is on the docket at the Supreme Court. The Senate judiciary committee has asked me to testify next month. They're conducting an investigation into the prosecution's conduct at your trial. Please, just give the process a little more time —

JAMAL HASSIM: There is no more time, Donald. There is no more time. [Pause] I can hear her crying, "Do not fail to honor what has been prescribed."

BRAND: Is Ahn saying this to you?

JAMAL HASSIM: She comes to me whenever I close my eyes.

* * *

Aseelah —

Dearest heart, blessed child. I am writing to let you know I am still alive. Not to be able to see you is an open wound, I am missing you so much. It is a daily struggle to keep myself from giving up. I can't sleep. I'm always hungry. I'm so alone and terrified; sometimes I think it would be better just to die.

What keeps me going is the thought of you, and the knowledge

*that judgment belongs only to God. In His name, and all that is holy,
I have resisted their attempts to make me say what is not true. The
truth is the only thing I have left, and I have not willingly allowed
them to take that away. But I now fear that guile has fostered what
force could not produce. A situation occurred a few weeks ago that
causes me to believe my resolve was compromised by a chemical
agent. I say this because of events surrounding an interrogation
shortly after I received what I was told was an inoculation for the flu.
I can only remember small pieces of it. It is very hazy, but I vaguely
remember accusations that struck me as negative toward your father,
to which I might have agreed. I do recall correcting myself at some
point, and renouncing what had been said — But I have no distinct
recollection what that was, and no way to assure myself these statements were suppressed. What makes me more uneasy is that after
months of interrogations — often twice a day — after this last session
there have suddenly been no more. It makes me think they finally
got what they were after, which is why they've gone away.*

*Aseelah, if you get this letter publish it immediately, and share it
with the world. Please tell anyone who will listen that I would never
intentionally say that your father or I were knowingly involved in a
plot to harm anyone. Let them know that we are innocent, and that
this is all a terrible mistake — which I believe began because we
called the FBI. Please let them know this. It might be our only
chance. You are brave and you are strong. Our lives are in your
hands —*

Side A
4/10/09

Yeah. I saw it.

I picked it up on my home page. Fuckin' headline of the *Financial Times*.

"Orphan from the War on Terror gets smuggled message from her mother. Alleges use of 'truth serums' to manipulate testimony. A charge the Justice Department vehemently denies."

I was just sayin' to Candy this is what happens when you rely on a bunch of gooks and postal inspectors to watch out for your interests. I mean, it's postmarked Manila and addressed to the daughter of a terrorist.

Do you need any more of a hint?

Hello!

And then they forward it no less!

That's the worst part.

You're right.

This should have been a routine foreign intelligence collection.

I don't care what kind of protections, under the law.

Hey, is it true what I hear — that the FBI is on its way right now to take the letter away from the kid?

Yeah, well I don't know why they didn't do that yesterday, before she read it on the evening news and got herself entrenched.

So once you get it, then what?

You'll file it in a secure facility, with a rating of highly sensitive national security information — subject to great scrutiny and a battery of tests.

Okay.

And then you'll challenge the authenticity with some of your in-house experts.

Say it's a forgery.

That the whole thing is a lie.

An underhanded defense tactic to offset the jailhouse confession Brandy says can't be used as evidence, 'cause his client's lost his mind.

I don't know, Fitzie, that's gonna be a tough sell now that the kid's got twenty-four hours on ya.

I mean, you can give it a try.

Alls I'm sayin' is that it ain't gonna be easy to retail, with all that commentary comin' out of the Hill, about this potentially evolving into all kinds of investigations.

I mean, I know you guys are as good as anyone at establishing a storyline, but when you got a situation like this, internally speaking, it's gotta be handled with an extra modicum of delicacy.

From a personal viewpoint, I would find someone who's informed enough to make 'em guilty, who ain't knowledgeable enough to be a danger to you.

I'd be lookin' toward Lossman for an assignment like that.

He'll be good to chum the pool.

I'd offer him some behind-the-scenes sweetheart deal, then publicly call on him to resign. That way when all them questions come up about what happened during the interrogation, he agrees to fall on his sword and say somethin' like, "I didn't see nothin' unusual when they was interviewing her. But if there's any fault, it's mine."

That's my Karl Rove opinion on one possible method of escape.

I know it's more complicated than that, what with all the questions being asked about the rendition...

and the new confessions...

and the missing tape.

That's why you need to throw Lossman in as an opening dona-tion. That'll give you some time to build in distance, and keep your head above the fray. Maybe consult with your shredder before them assholes in Congress start asking for documents that might be too sensitive to be sending up and —

Wait.

What?

How do I shine into this?

The U.S Attorney wants me to make myself available personally for when questions come up about my involvement the case?

Did she forget that asking me to do that could potentially put my life at risk?

I don't care what kind of hotel accommodations under what assumed name.

You tell her I'm gonna need better built-in protections than that before I agree to come back to the States.

I'm thinking total immunity from any past or future crimes.

A raise in my monthly allowance — and a new name under the witness protection program. Which, after all I've done for her, is about time.

Oh, is that right?

Under the circumstances there can't be any special dispensa-tions.

I suggest you go back and advise against that position.

Oh, really?

That's not in your purview?

Well then, let me put something in front of you that is, for lack of a better word, a little bit of an appetizer that may give your boss a more discretionary attitude.

See, you may think you made a commitment, but commitment is the wrong word. What you made was a projection when you said, "We got to get Conner back to New York 'cause now that we're under a little bit of a microscope his conduct could potentially give us a black eye. So we'll bring him back under the guise of bein' a trusted compatriot — meanwhile, we'll secretly indict."

See, you might be able to pull that with some of them Afghan drug lords who think they have a superlative relationship until they run out of colleagues to contribute, after which the onus gets put on their head.

Meaning, this is strictly a relationship of mutual expedience.

In that, once we got all we can get, we're gonna change the objective, which may not conform to the agreed-upon end.

So I can understand how your boss might be tempted to say, "Now that this situation has made Conner a little bit of a hot potato, we have no choice but to light him up for securities fraud, and get his other sentence underway." At least then when we have to testify in front of Congressman Muckety-Muck and Senator So-and-So, we can say, "Yes, it's an embarrassment, but as soon as we discovered the problem, we took appropriate action."

If I were her, that's what I'd be lookin' at, 'cause what we have here is a mirror image of ourselves.

But that ain't the only way this situation should be looked at — and I say this to you as a brother, 'cause we're joined at the hip — like them Siamese Twins that share liver and a heart from a communal point of view —

What was that?

I shouldn't mention myself in the same breath?

The same breath as who?

Are you callin' from your office?

Good. 'Cause I want you to open your file cabinet and take a look under "F."

No, I'm not thinking of Farley, although, if I don't say so myself, that one was a beaut. A hundred and thirty seven months for wire fraud, tax fraud, mail fraud, and corruption. I don't think we'll be seein' him back at the State House again any time soon. Do you?

But that's not what we're lookin' for.

No, no not Finkleman either. That stupid son of a bitch, sending me home with my Rolex, then mailing the box to my cousin in Philly.

That's not the one I had in mind.

And not Fleishman either. Even though he was one of my all time favorites, Rabbi Fleishman. Sixty-eight months for laundering charity donations.

That was the best!

No, no. That's not it, though.

The one I'm thinking of is deeper in the alphabet.

Ahhh, I knew you'd find it, 'cause you're a quick one, Fitzie.

That's riiiight.

The file labeled "Fuck You."

You see it?

Open it up and take a look inside.

Just about now I'm bettin' that all them subpoenaed inter-office e-mails don't look so scary no more.

And you can relay to your boss I got more where that comes from.

I've been recording since 1995.

It's like I always say to Candy, "You can be all kissy-face when you're negotiating, but until everything's signed off on and sealed, words don't mean squat."

So go back to your boss and tell her to make sure I get a good 5K1 letter.

You know, the kind that says, "No jail time for Conner."

And while you're at it, tell her to slide me into another service, now that workin' for you guys is too hot.

After she does that, and gets me immunity, I'll think about disclosing where the masters are, in which numbered accounts.

Until then she can spend the rest of her days wondering when I'm gonna let the other shoe drop.

* * *

Thank you, Mr. Chairman.

We turn now to the U.S. Attorney for the Southern District of New York, Margarita M. Ney. Ms. Ney has held the office of U.S. Attorney in the Southern District of New York for seven years. During that time she has been involved in many high-profile prosecutions of terrorist and white-collar crimes, notwithstanding the case against Jamal Hassim, which we have called this hearing to discuss today. Before that, she worked as an assistant U.S. Attorney for five years, with a ninety-eight percent conviction rate. She graduated from Georgetown University with a bachelor's degree, and went from there to Harvard Law. She was a partner at the esteemed firm of Conyers, Dunlevy, and Black in New York before accepting a position in government service.

We have allotted twenty minutes for your opening statement, Ms. Ney, because of the complexity and importance of the issues which you and we will be addressing.

You may proceed.

NEY: Good morning Mr. Chairman, and members of the Judiciary Committee. I'm pleased to have this opportunity to speak with you today. And let me just add for the record that when the Chairman asked me if I would be willing to speak under oath, I said I would have no objection. I also said I would give the same answers to your questions whether or not my testimony was sworn.

As you mentioned in your opening speech, Mr. Chairman, in our America, no one is above the law. I want to assure this committee that the criminal prosecution of Jamal Hassim and all one hundred and thirty members of his North American terror cell has been conducted with utmost care and scrutiny, with great emphasis on the integrity of the evidence and the defendant's civil rights.

I'm not here to discuss operational details, or any other classified information that could endanger current military operations in the southern Philippines or the other prosecutions now currently underway that are related to this case. What I can say is that after an exhaustive internal investigation, I have been personally assured that outside of the accidental mishandling of Ahn Hassim's confession tape, no other irregularities associated with evidence gathered to support the prosecution of Jamal and Ahn Hassim have been found. Notwithstanding the Justice Department's finding that no intentional loss of evidence occurred, all government attorneys and FBI agents associated with this inadvertent lapse have offered to step down.

I would like to remind this panel that counterterrorism experts say that evidence gathered by the undercover operative in the Hassim case has been crucial in stopping what has been characterized as a quickly-developing organization of Islamic extremists from across Southeast Asia, who were in the process of assembling a new international force for jihad. In fighting the war on terrorism, government officials often have to engage informants with questionable backgrounds. As this case clearly illustrates, the help of such individuals has the potential to bring admitted terrorists like Jamal Hassim to justice, and save thousands of American lives.

Now, some have asked about the timing of the Defense Department's request to change Major Hassim's status from criminal defendant to enemy combatant. Let me respond to that concern by reminding you that such requests have occurred before, and assure you that the gravity of the situation demanded a quick and decisive response in the interest of national security. I know you appreciate the serious constraints on what I can say about the nature of the information that forced us to make the unprecedented decision to interrupt a federal trial. Unfortunately, much of that information continues to remain too sensitive to discuss in an open forum. However, as a matter of public confidence, I have been authorized to disclose that the attempted escape of Ahn Hassim from national police headquarters in Manila, and her subsequent death in a shootout with law enforcement authorities there, created concerns that a similar type of prison break might have been planned for her husband by Islamic terrorists in this country, particularly during periods of transport to and from the courtroom. This and oth —

HAPPENING NOW
U.S. AIRWAYS JET GOES DOWN OFF THE COAST OF NEW JERSEY

>> We interrupt this broadcast to report that a U.S. Airways 737 jet en route to Bangor, Maine has crashed just minutes after takeoff from Newark International Airport. There have been reports that the left engine was on fire shortly before it went down. We're going to switch over to our affiliates at **KMB TV** for more details...

>>Charlie, there's a lot of confusion here about what just happened. Some witnesses have reported that they saw a flare, or missile, strike the fuselage. These are unconfirmed accounts at this time, but I'm being told that the Department of Homeland Security has suspended all service to and from this airport as a precaution, until they can ascertain the cause of this horrific accident.

>> I'm just receiving information that law enforcement authorities are saying that someone in Teaneck has found what appears to be a shoulder-launched surface-to-air missile in the back of an abandoned pickup truck. Do you have any confirmation of that on your end?

>>I'm hearing similar reports. I've also just received word that the Coast Guard is headed toward the approximate location of the crash site, about six miles off the shore of Cape May.

>>Do they think there's any hope of finding survivors?

>>From what I'm told, there is little hope that any of the 219 passengers and five crew members will be found alive. We're hearing that the fuselage had broken into two or three separate pieces before impact. As you can imagine, it's just a horrible scene in the terminal right now, where many family members have gathered. Apparently, there were a large number of children on this flight, on their way to summer camp. FAA grief counselors are currently on their way to give support.

>> Okay, we're going to switch over to these pictures coming out of Washington, where an emergency evacuation of the Capitol is underway. There are people running everywhere as fast as they can. It's a very chaotic situation on the ground, and we have to assume that the government is concerned that what happened to U.S. Airways Flight 163 was not an accident, judging from this reaction. Wait a minute please...Oh, my God...

>>We've just received information that a United Airlines jet landing at Denver's International Airport has been shot down...

Tape 1A 10/13/10
Side A

[REDACTED]

Candy. Candy. Come on. You've got to get with the program.

Oh no, no, no. It's too late to be havin' second thoughts, 'cause this situation's already at the dock. You can't be cherry picking what you will and won't do at this juncture. You're committed to this whether you like it or not — which I don't know why you wouldn't be. This is our retirement that just pulled in. So try to relax and have some fun. This is gonna be like shootin' into a barrel of fish.

What I'm saying is, there's already a high level of interest on the other side.

Meaning, where you're going to take the wife for dinner tonight should be the only reservation on your mind.

This is our road to super wealth.

So give 'em a wave, and that cute synthetic smile.

Perfect. It's a beautiful scene.

Now just play along and follow my lead.

I'm gonna eat this guy up for us. Then, we're set for life.

[RESUME]

Dr. Shariq! You're looking mighty dapper!

My captain tells me you and the wife enjoyed your lobsters outside.

No doubt about it.

Dubai City makes a great backdrop view.

Especially from the deck of a hundred and twenty foot Fedship.

Hey, after we get done with this deal, I'll give you the name of my broker.

Maybe you want to buy one too.

Or a house like this in Moscow. I'll tell ya, it's a perfect situation. You got a golf course, tennis courts, a private marina — a tax free zone for business. I mean, what's not to like?

Where else can you travel the globe in less than a day?

That's what I told the Mrs. when she was pushin' to live on Palm Island.

To which I says, not for nothin', but why live on the trunk of a tree when you could own half of Brazil?

This way you can take one of them water taxis to New York or Los Angeles if you ever find yourself missing the States, which I don't know why you would when there's more Chanel here than there is in Paris — which is only a boat ride away.

So she settled for this estate in Rostov. And let me tell ya, it wasn't an easy sell, 'cause she swore she'd never live in Russia, even with an acre of prime beachfront on the Arabian Gulf.

But, it's like I've been known to say, why get up in arms about which city you live in or what continent it's on, when they're all surrounded by the same breakwater anyways?

And it works out perfectly, 'cause there ain't nobody here but a few odd sheiks that ain't in from out of town — which gives me the ability to give characters like you another layer of insulation to enrich your situation — and put some extra fissile on your plate. Which couldn't be better, since I'm very efficient at creating situations that remotely pass muster, from a compliance point of view.

Nice and quiet, under the radar.

Where no one knows from nothin', 'til the cow's way outta the barn, and there's nothin' they can do.

And, perplexingly enough, I'm very friendly with other very creative entities in this little corner of the universe. You'll see what I mean when we cruise back this evening to meet with one of my colleagues for some raucous activity in the entertainment zone.

This is a very near and dear friend, with a half a billion in his discretionary account.

He's one of us with a Persian accent.

Okay?

In addition, I've bonded telephonically with a plethora of potential investors who are eminently capable of participating in this venture, with a large propensity to play.

Which is why I says to bin Phoeben, "This is clever shit. It smells good, and it's packaged beautifully. I need to see this guy on a private basis before he goes back to Damascus and proliferates through a bunch of sub-cretins running a bullshit subsidiary outta some armpit in Oman..."